CAUGHT UP IN A DOPEBOY'S LOVE 2

GABRIELA AND LEGEND'S STORY

A NOVEL BY

CARMEN LASHAY

CONTENTS

Title Page	
Published by Carmen Lashay	2
ACKNOWLEDGEMENTS	3
PREVIOUSLY ON CAUGHT UP IN A DOPEBOY'S LOVE	7
LEGEND	8
GABRIELA	17
GABRIELA	56
LEGEND	81
CREAM	108
STACY	116
CASE	129
TOO BE CONTINUED....	167

PUBLISHED BY CARMEN LASHAY

ALL RIGHTS RESERVED

ANY unauthorized reprint or use of the material is prohibited. No part of this book may be reproduced or transmitted in any form or by any means, electronic, or mechanical, including photocopying, recoding, or by any information storage without express permission by the author. This is the original work of fiction. Names, characters, places and incidents are either products of the author's imagination or are used fictitiously an any resemblance to actual person's living or dead, is entirely coincidental.

Contains explicit language & adult themes suitable for ages 16+only.

ACKNOWLEDGE-MENTS

First, I want to take time out to give thanks to God, who is forever the head of my life. With Him, all things are possible. As always, I would like to take a few moments and give thanks to a few people whom I love, admire, and that hold a special place in my heart. They go above and beyond to make this journey I'm walking an easy one for me with just the support they display.

To my parents, whom I love dearly, I want to thank you for just loving me and raising such a strong-willed and motivated young lady. Know that I am everything that I am because of you guys. Both of you continuously pushed me to be the best me I could be, and you taught me a very valuable lesson at a young age. It doesn't matter that you were knocked down. It's the fact that you got back up that counts.

To my wonderful husband Paul Smith II who is always my number one fan, thank you for encouraging me daily to reach for the skies in the pursuit of my dreams.

To my sister, Paulesha Hill, I thank you for staying on me when I wanted to give up and motivating me to keep pushing forward. I also thank you for always encouraging me to keep going when I start to doubt myself. I am so glad that I returned the favor and pushed and motivated you to also pursue your writing dreams! I want everyone reading this to go check out her catalog! Trust me! I love you times a million and know that whatever road in life you choose to walk, you'll never walk it alone.

To the wonderfully amazing Wendy Jenkins, I thank you for always being there when I need you to bounce ideas off of, and you give me your honest opinion. With so many pinned stories, and taking on some many different tasks at once besides writing, I sometimes feel like I'm losing my way, but you are always there to read over my work for me giving me your honest opinion of a story line and really walking this path with me making my book come alive. I appreciate you more than you will ever know.

To my longtime best friend, Keiaira Cooper, who is always there for me no matter what time it is, you always read each and every book I write and put up with me during my meltdown moments. Our sessions always give me a burst of energy and motivation.

To Latherio Kidd and Lei, I love you guys to pieces, and knowing you are in my corner, rooting me on, makes me want to go even harder with this pen! Last but certainly not least, I want to acknowledge you, the readers. Without you, I wouldn't be motivated to drop book after book. Writing is something I love doing, and I find it very therapeutic. When I write, I can see the characters playing out in my mind like a movie that pauses when I take a break and plays when I start back up.

LAST BY CERTAINLY NOT LEAST, I want to thank each and every one of you who takes time out of your day to read my books, whether it be an e-book copy or a paperback one. Thank you for that. I also love reading reviews from you guys, good or bad. I like your honest feedback, and I promise I take everything into consideration each time I write a new book. My dream is to go all the way to the top, and I'm taking each and every one of you with me. I love you bunches, and I can't say it enough.

In loving memory of my grandmother, Eddie Lee Bell, my cousin, Willisha "Lisha" Miller, and my step father, Anthony Baker. Gone but never forgotten. Everything that I do, I do in memory of you

SYNOPSIS

They say real hittas don't die, they just multiply, but is that the case with Legend? After that chilling end to part one, who will be left standing when the smoke clears? This explosive second installment picks up right where it left off with steamy drama and more chaos than you can imagine. The question is, did Gabriela and Legend manage to survive? And if they did, where does their love story go from here now that Legend knows Silas is Gabriela's uncle?

Young, wild, and reckless, Stacy liked to consider herself the female version of a man. She played by her own rules and lived life her way. She didn't have a boyfriend that she could call her own, and didn't desire one either, was the lie she liked to tell herself. It was really her unwillingness to put her heart back on the line that made it impossible for her to keep a man. Omarion said it best when he sang about an ice box being where his heart used to be because that's exactly how Stacy viewed men and love. That is until she met Cream in Jamaica. So used to men fighting for her love, Stacy was both intrigued and annoyed at Cream's nonchalant attitude when it came to her. Will she throw caution to the wind, tell him how she feels, and see where things could lead? Or will her stubbornness cause her to miss out on a real chance at love?

Cream best friend and right hand man to Legend likes to consider himself a loner. He appears when he's needed, and stays out of the way when he's not. Quiet, silent and deadly, the mysterious Cream is the type that takes no shit and doesn't have time for the games and drama that relationships bring. He's content with bedding them, leaving them, and moving on the next with no feelings attached; until he meets Stacy. Even though she's everything he doesn't like in a woman, loud, ghetto, and untamable, he still finds himself drawn to her. Unable to determine ifs it's love or lust, will Cream still take a chance on Stacy or will her stubborn ways cause him to lose interest and move on.

Strap back in for another explosive action packed ride with Gabriela, Legend, Stacy, and Cream as they all battle through sex, lies, deceit, and enemy's at every corner in this heart pounding mind blowing series. Will Gabriela finally get to mend her broken heart and find her happily ever after? Or will she once again bite off more than she can chew getting Caught up in a DopeBoys love 2.

PREVIOUSLY ON CAUGHT UP IN A DOPEBOY'S LOVE

LEGEND

"So tell me again how it is that two of my trap houses were hit?" I asked slamming my hands down on the table. I was in the middle of handling business trying to secure a new plug Cream hit my line saying two of our traps got hit. I knew without even having to investigate that it was Silas ass. That's the only nigga we had beef with right now even though he had been quiet for a while now but I damn sure wasn't sleeping on the nigga, I just couldn't find him. He had gotten smart and moved his momma as well and disappeared off the grid.

"The shit happened so fast, we was caught off guard," one of the men said.

"And what you was doing when niggas was catching bullets?"

"A nigga had a gun to my head, I couldn't do shit," dude said.

"Damn a whole gun to your head? Like this?" I asked walking up on him pulling my gun out.

"Yeah," he said.

"So when you felt that steel on you, instead of protecting my shit with your life, you went out like a bitch and let my shit get took?" I asked.

"Man it wasn't like that. I got a family," was all I let him get out before I blew his brains out. One by one whoever was still alive from the break in got put down. They should have died with them other niggas or at least took a few bullets. That would have let me know they at least tried to do something. These niggas was sitting here giving me fucking excuses, and didn't have not one scratch on them.

"I need all my lieutenants to lock everything up, we shutting down for the next few days," I said.

"Next few days, we gone lose a lot of bread," I heard a few of them say.

"Nigga I know what the fuck y'all gone lose, I said lock the shit down. In the meantime go home, and spend time with your family because when we open back up, everybody moving the fuck in the traps for a while. Since y'all can't make sure my shit secure, y'all all gone protect that shit with your life. I don't give a fuck how y'all do it, where y'all sleep, and how y'all work that shit out, but I bet y'all won't let this shit happen again," I said walking off without saying another word.

"What you got planned today?" Cream asked me catching up to me.

"I had a few moves to make, but ima chill out today. I need to really sit down with Gabriela so we can work shit out and be on the same page as far as what we doing," I said. I had been fucking with her heavy these last few days, and shit now she wanted a nigga to meet her pops and shit. I mean I knew I liked her, but I also wasn't rushing into anything right now. With the way my life was so hectic dealing with bullshit everything time I turned around; I knew that wasn't something I wanted to subject her to. But shit I also couldn't go long without being near her and slept better when she slept under me. Shit it's like I was playing tug of war with my feelings at this point, so shit I had to figure this shit out and fast.

"Nigga you sick or some shit?" Cream asked me.

"What? Nigga naw I ain't sick. Why would I be sick?"

"Since when you give a fuck about sitting down working shit out?"

"Since I found out I was gone be a dad. I'm telling you fuck what any bitch made ass nigga say, the minute you find out you about to bring another life into this world, that shit dead ass changes you," I said.

"Shit I feel that. Man I can't even imagine your ass as being somebody daddy."

"You know I love kids; I can't wait. I want a son so his little can be fresh as soon as he slide out the pussy. My lil nigga gone have all the nursery room babies on his dick," I said as Cream shook his head laughing.

"Damn I hope Gabriela know what she getting herself into with your crazy ass."

"She probably don't, but ima lay it all out on the table today and we can go from there," I said. I didn't mean I was gone tell her ass all about my illegal dealings and shit like that. I just meant me as a person. I got short patience, no tolerance for bullshit you know shit along those lines.

"Why you ain't asked her to take a look into your brother's case yet?" Cream said saying what I had been thinking ever since the judge again denied bail and it looked like my lawyer basically was just bullshitting around at this point. To be so young, Gabby seemed to be good at what she did. I looked into her and saw she played no games in this courtroom. Even though she quit her job didn't mean she couldn't still practice law. She would be a good asset to my team, I just needed to know I could trust her first because I would hate for our child to grow up motherless.

"Like I said, I'm not going too deep into shit tonight, but I'm laying it all on the tables, and we gone go from there. You know me, it's always a method to my madness.

****

The ringing of my phone woke me up. After I had left the warehouse, I swung by my crib, checked on shit that way, got my mail, grabbed some more clothes, than came back to Gabby crib. I would have never guessed I would actually be comfortable enough to lay my head in a crib that wasn't mines. I still carried my gun around, and had a few stashed throughout her house, but that was mainly about being smart, and ready for whatever.

Anyway, since I noticed she still wasn't back from the mall yet, I had laid across the bed to take a quick nap.
My phone continuing to ring jolted me fully awake as I noticed it was my mother calling me. Sitting up, I answered it,

"Hello."

"Julian mi yaad pan fire"(Julian my house is on fire)my mother said into the phone as I sat up.

"What? wah yuh mean yuh yaad pan fire? yuh ok(What? What do you mean your house is on fire? Are you ok) I said panicked as I sat up. She went on to tell me that she had been away at my aunt Olivia's house, Quan and Mike's momma, consoling her because she had a nervous breakdown. She had lost her husband and both of her sons and apparently wasn't doing too well. My mother had been staying with her a few days.

"Mi leave mi neighba Elizabeth here tuh yaad sit fi mi an mi tink shi still inside." (I left my neighbor Elizabeth here to house sit for me and I think she still inside)

"Who all kno yuh did gone?" (Who all knew you was gone?)

"Nobody." She said.

"Gud don't call di babylon let everybody tink yuh inside of di yaad tek a Uba tuh a hotel room," I said(Good, don't call the police. Let everybody think you are inside of the house. Take an Uber to a hotel room)

"But," she started to protest until cut her off.

"Don't argue wid mi ma duh as mi sey an guh Send mi di name pan di hotel wen yuh get there an inna di meantime mi a wuk pan getting yaah passport mi should ave been put mi foot dung an had yuh here wid mi."(Don't argue with me ma, do as I say and go. Send me the name on the hotel when you get there and in the meantime ima work on getting you a passport. I should have been put my foot down and had you here with me.)

"But jamaica a mi home." (But jamaica is my home)

"Yuh nuh safe there right now an mi can't protect yuh from here guh now ma don't mek mi haffi hop a plane." (You not safe there right now and I can't protect you from here. Go now ma, don't make me have to hop a plane) I said hanging up the phone as I cursed and fucked shit in the room forgetting I wasn't at my own house. I knocked over lamps and punched a hole in the wall as I dialed up Tan.

"Hello?"

"I need you to look into getting my mom a passport to the

United States with overnight delivery. I don't care what we have to pay, make that happen and get back to me ASAP," I said hanging up without even giving her a chance to speak. Next, I called a number and after the fifth ring, the caller finally answered.

"Let me speak to Case," I said to the Co I had on payroll. She had Case's phone and to keep it from getting took during pat downs, she kept it on her.

"You know he can't talk right now, I'm not even in his pod right now it's another guard over there. Call him back in a few hours," she said.

"Listen bitch I don't give a fuck what time it is and who is where, I do know I not only pay for your daughter high ass college tuition, but that mortgage on that big ass house you living in. If you wanna keep that house, your life, and your kids life, you'll put my damn brother on this phone right the fuck now!" I barked. I was slowly losing my cool because somebody just tried to kill my mother and I had to check and make sure Case was straight. The phone went silent for a few minutes before I heard,

"Yo what's up?" Case said. I let out a breath I didn't even realize I was holding in.

"You straight bro?"

"Hell naw the food in this bitch sucks, I need a steak or some shit," Case said.

"Man listen you need to keep your eyes open and pay attention to your surroundings. The candy lady mad somebody stole their candy and they crazy asses tried to burn somebody momma house down. She wasn't in it though, I'm sure it made the news," I said talking in code letting him know Silas tried to burn the house down with ma in it.

"What!" He yelled.

"Calm down, I'ma handle shit on this end, you just keep your eyes open and have them niggas in their doing around the clock watch. I know shit about to get crazy because I'm about to give this nigga the war he just asked for."

"I'm ready for whatever that comes my way, they gone know that Santiago boys ain't shit to play with. They want me dead, they *gotta work it,"* Case said making me smile like a proud parent.

"Ima get you up out that bitch soon bruh but damn straight make them bitches put in over time! Put anything down that blinks wrong. Remember what I always told you, sleeping on a nigga will get you slept. One love keep your head up, I got you back,"

"Until that casket drops," he finished before disconnecting the call. The minute he hung up; I called my mother back as I texted Tan at the same time.

"Hail?" (Hello) she said.

"Mi tink mi tell yuh tuh call mi di second yuh get tuh di room," (I thought I told you to call me the second you got to the room) I said to her.

"I'm just checking inna Julian I'm at di Marriot an mi did text yuh di hotel name." (I'm just checking in Julian. I'm at the Marriot and I did text you the hotel name)

"Cut up all yuh credit cards mi just wired sum funds inna a offshore account an mi ave men heading tuh yuh hotel as wi speak dat wi tek yuh fi get clothes an oddah things you'll need fi di room while yuh there Don't worry dem won't lef yuh side." (Cut up all your credit cards. I just wired some money into an offshore account and I have men heading to your hotel as we speak that will take you to get clothes and other things you'll need for the room while you are there. Don't worry they won't leave your side) I said to her texting away on my phone. I made sure I had somebody hack into the hotel database and erase any trace of my mother checking in, and of her taking an uber. I was also pep talking my men making sure them niggas I had on payroll in Jamaica knew how serious I was when I said they better protect my momma with their life because their families lives depended on it.

"What's gwaan Julian (What's going on Julian)

"Di less yuh kno di betta It should be men outside yuh doa now let dem inna fi mi an den hand dem di phone." (The less you know the better. It should be men outside your door now, let them in for me and then hand them the phone)

"Ok." She said as I heard the door open. A few seconds later, I heard Rootie speak into the phone.

"Guard her with y'all life bruh, that's my heart. Y'all got one job," I did.

"You know we got you Legend, you always look out for us on our end making sure we still eating," he said which was true I made sure every nigga on my team ate even if I didn't immediately need their services.

"Tell her to lay down and get some rest. Keep me posted and I will hit you back in a few," I said. Hanging up, I called Tan back,

"You found a way to get her an overnight passport?"

"If she already had a passport, she could have paid for an overnighted one. But, for new passports, the earliest I'm finding is a week," she said.

"Bribe whoever you gotta bribe, but legally or illegally I need her here tomorrow Tan," I said again hanging up. I quickly texted Cream putting him on game as I jumped up and quickly grabbing my stuff up so I could get in these streets. I wanted to kill this nigga so damn bad I could taste it, but first, I had to make sure my moms and Case was straight. Putting on my shoes, I sent Gabriela a text telling her that her play date was over it was time for her to come home. As a matter of fact when she got back, I was taking her to my crib because it was definitely more lowkey and secure than this place.

Checking to make sure I had my keys, I ran down the steps, and threw the front door open only to come face to face with none other than Silas as I saw a car door closing and another man walking towards the door. Then it hit me, **"I'll take everything you love and everything you never got the chance to love."** Silas words played back in my mind as I realized he really was talking about Gabriela, and he knew about the baby. I didn't know how his ass knew, but he did, and as calculated as I was, and how I was always one step ahead of niggas, since earlier, this nigga been catching me slipping all damn day.

Maybe allowing myself to love Gabriela possibly threw me off my square. I was the main nigga always yelling about how niggas always slip up when they get a bitch, and look how the fuck I just did the same thing. Knowing I wasn't going out like no damn sucker, I did the only other rational thing I could think of, I punched this nigga dead *in his shit and we started going blow for blow as we somehow made our way fully into the house throwing each other into the walls and shit really fucking shit up. To be an old ass nigga, his ass was hanging with me but I was getting the best of him.*

"What the fuck," I heard the nigga who came with him say as he tried to break us up but neither one of us was going. Somehow though, he managed to get us apart, and soon as we broke apart, I reached for my gun immediately drawing it on him at the same time as he pulled a gun out on my ass as well. I had another gun in the back of my jeans, if I died right now, I knew I would go down fighting, and I was definitely taking this bitch nigga with me.

"Bout time you dropped yo nuts and came to see me like a man ole bitch ass nigga. You been pulling bitch shit all damn day. You better hope I die because ima enjoy chopping your mothers old ass up into little pieces. Just for the fun of it, ima snatch her dentures out and cut them bitches up as well. However, before I start chopping on her wrinkle body ass, ima have a doctor on standby to make sure her heart doesn't give out until the very end," I said.

"Well too bad you won't be making it out of here then. And I handle all my shit myself bitch nigga, you the only one keep trying to get at my family but won't step to me," he said as I looked at his funny looking ass with confusion. I never went after nobody in his damn family, yet.

"I don't know what's going on here and I don't give a fuck, I'm not the one to fuck with," dude finally spoke up.

"You can die with this bitch ass nigga." I said to him pulling another gun out that I had tucked in the back of my jeans. I was done with the talking and was ready to get shit cracking when I heard,

"What the hell is going on in here?" As I saw Gabriela walking into the house. Instantly my entire mood changed as my focus went to her and my child. I didn't know how I would get them out of here, but I for damn sure would die trying.

"Gabriela what the fuck is going on?" Silas and the man said to her at the same time. It's like deju was happening to me all over again but instead of her being like Myriah fucking my best friend, she had played the game even more raw. She was fucking with the

enemy. Damn. I just couldn't catch a break with this love shit.

"I don't know myself. Julian put that gun down," she said all innocently which enraged me. Quickly turning one of my guns on her, I said.

"You little bitch you setting me up huh!" I yelled.

"What are you talking about? I'm not setting anybody up," she said as the nigga who was with Silas quickly moved in front of her. I smirked when I saw this. At this point, all of us was about to die in this bitch because everybody in this room had me fucked up right now.

"You not setting me up but you fucking with Silas? Yeah fuck you and that baby bitch," I said cocking my gun back.
"Wait I told you about Silas earlier. I told you my father and my uncle Bo were stopping by to meet you. Uncle Bo's real is Silas," she screamed just as me and Silas both squeezed the trigger at the same time.

POW! POW! POW!

GABRIELA

POW!POW!

As the sound of guns went off, I closed my eyes and immediately felt myself go deaf as my father instantly threw me to the ground; I heard even more bullets rang out. I knew Julian told me he was crazy; I just didn't know he was actually this crazy! Like where did he even get a gun from? And I didn't even know my Uncle Bo owned a gun either! When my father threw me to the ground, I fell on a turned over table hitting my head and the side of my stomach hard as hell as all the sound in the room seemed to turn off instantly.

Not only couldn't I hear anything, but now all I felt was an excruciating pain shooting up my body that caused me to scream out in pain. I opened my eyes to see my father standing over me saying something, I just couldn't hear him because my ears were still ringing from the guns going off. I closed my eyes again and balled up into a tight ball as I again screamed out in pain as tears ran rapidly down my face. This day had officially gone from bad to worse in a matter of minutes. First, CoCo threw me for a loop when she said Chanel was the one who was sleeping with Chance in my house all along. I stood there laughing because I didn't believe the hoe.

A bitter ass female like that would always make something up just to hurt you like they were hurting. However, when instead of Chanel laughing as well, denying it and putting CoCo's ass in her place for even insinuating some shit like that, she put her head down. My heart dropped to the pits of my stomach because I instantly knew it wasn't a lie. Apparently so did my friends because before I could blink, Stacy had kicked the security guard holding her in the balls as he released her and doubled over in pain. She then ran full force into Chanel who wasn't expecting that because Stacy pounced on her like a lion attacking its prey. Hell even Destiny hauled off and got a lick in. The entire time I just stood there still in shock as CoCo and her ugly ass friends laughed and walked away.

Meanwhile the police showed up and arrested Stacy, while the ambulance had to be called for Chanel because she was even more fucked up when Stacy got finished with her than she was when CoCo attacked her. I had planned on coming home telling Julian about everything that had happened since he texted me right as I was talking to an officer saying that I needed to come home right away. I never imagined I would walk into another war zone though!

"Where does it hurt?" My father asked me feeling gently all over my stomach as my hearing slowly came back as I started to understand his questions.

"Bitch ass nigga, this what you meant when you said you would take everything I never got a chance to love, bitch you was planning on killing your own niece right along with my child and my momma? You gotta kill me first bitch," I heard Julian yell followed by a lot of scuffling and commotion.

"Nigga I would never fucking hurt my damn niece! I wasn't talking about her nor my future godchild. It's something else yo ass will never get a chance to love," I heard my Uncle Boo say followed by glass breaking.

"What's going on daddy make them stop," I screamed trying to sit up as I felt something trickling down my head. I lifted my hand up touching it and noticed it was blood as I screamed out.

"My fucking child over here hurt and damn near bleeding to death and you two muthafuckas still in here trying to kill each other," my father yelled as it seemed like all the commotion instantly stopped.

"Fuckkkk," I heard someone yell out but I couldn't make out who it was. The yell was following by a loud noise.

"This nigga punching holes in walls and shit, bitch ass nigga this all your fucking fault," I heard who I thought I was certain was my Uncle Boo.

"Sit up for me baby. This blood getting all over your face," my father said as he took his shirt off wiping my face with it.

"I just hit Emily up, her and doc on the way and should be here any minute now. Get her some water Los," Uncle Bo said as I struggled to sit up. Once I was up, I frantically looked around for Julian who I didn't see anywhere. I didn't know where he had disappeared to that fast because I know I had heard his voice moments ago. It's crazy because even though he fired an actual real loaded gun towards my direction, I still wanted him here with me right now.

"Where did Julian go?" I asked barely even recognizing my own voice right as I held the top of my head.
"He lets you call him Julian? Yeah he milking this bullshit ass act huh?" Uncle Bo said.

"Fuck that nigga, he shot at you, and shot your uncle. That's who the fuck you made a baby with? A bitch ass nigga like that?" My father asked me looking both concerned and disappointed. It's like I couldn't win for losing with him because instead of him seeing the person I saw every day, he had to witness a different side of Julian; the side he warned me I didn't want to see.

"I didn't shoot at her ass cuz if I did, I wouldn't have missed. I ain't never missed a target in my life, if I wanted to pop her ass I would have. It's y'all niggas that had me fucked up. Her father and uncle or not, ain't no nigga gone try me," I heard an angry Julian say as I looked up kind of relived to see him. I didn't even realize I had been more concerned about him than my Uncle Bo until I noticed him bleeding as well.

"Uncle Bo you're bleeding!" I said trying to get up but the pain that shot through my entire body forced me to stay exactly where I was.

"I'm ok baby girl it's gone take more than a bullet to put me down. Don't try and move my doc on the way," he said before turning back to Julian who was busy dumping items out of my purse and tearing old case files of mines up.

"This ain't over bitch ass nigga. Ima see your ass again," Uncle Bo said.

"Not if I see you first pussy! This doesn't change shit for me my nigga! Ima comfort her ass after you get put to sleep," Julian said as he limped over in my direction. It was then that I realized he was bleeding as well.

"Everybody needs to calm down! Julian you can't talk to my uncle nor father like that! What's wrong with you! How do you guys even know each other and why are you so angry with one another? Look at this place, you guys destroyed my house! Mine! I paid for this shit; I worked my ass off for this shit! You guys in here behaving like some adolescent teenagers! Look at you guys, both bleeding, y'all need a hospital," I frantically said again trying to stand up, but again falling right back down. This was a nightmare that I desperately wanted to wake up from. All the men I loved in my life where in the same room together but it wasn't the happy gathering I had envisioned this moment being.

"Fuck that nigga, we out," Julian said finally making it over to where I was.

"Nigga I don't know what you and Silas got going on and I don't give a fuck! This my baby, my heart, and I won't play about her ass. All them empty ass threats you been throwing out you can save that shit! You better do your research on Los young nigga! Make me come the fuck out of retirement if you wanna!" My father said as he stood up blocking Julian from getting to me.

"Shit come out then nigga! I was in retirement as well until a bitch nigga decided to bring my ass out too now everybody gotta feel me! But check this out, I don't give a fuck bout what you talking about right now my nigga, what I do know is this fucking house is hot and the laws on their way! While you two niggas was busy down here talking and shit, I'm the one been ramp sacking shit making it look like somebody ran up in this bitch looking for a file or something and fucked her up. Lawyers get hurt all the time from old cases! So y'all can stay y'all dumb ass here waiting for a fucking doctor and talk to the pigs if you want to and explain all this shit to them. In the meantime I'm taking my baby momma and my seed to the doctor because that's the only thing in this bitch I give a fuck about!" Julian said as he pushed past my father who didn't put up an effort to stop him.

I wanted to protest and yell at him for again talking to my father in that tone, but at the moment I was starting to feel lightheaded and didn't have much of any fight in me left. I gave him a weak smile as he stood in front of me but instead of him returning it, he gave me the coldest look I've ever seen from him. I was innocent in all of this so I didn't understand why he was directing his anger at me as well. Bending down, he picked me up like I wasn't big as hell and carrying another person inside of me. As he was turning around to head towards the door, my father again blocked his path as they both had an intense stare down.

"Take care of my baby, her mother died bringing her into this world, and I'll die to make sure she stays here," my father said. Instead of Julian saying anything back, he simply nodded his head.

"Los you really gone let this bitch ass nigga leave with baby girl," Uncle Bo said.

"Try and stop me nigga and we gone have some problems," Julian said.

"Let him go Silas, he not gone hurt her."

"I'm ok Uncle Bo," I said trying to reassure him.

"No you not, not with this nigga. I don't know how he found you but don't worry, I'm shutting all this shit down now. Your fight is with me bitch ass nigga so leave my niece out of this," Uncle Bo said.

"Like you left my momma out of it huh?" Julian said.

"Nigga I ain't touch yo damn momma, and I damn sure ain't send nobody at her head. It don't matter how many men I got behind me, I handles shit myself pussy," Uncle Bo said.

"I don't feel so good," I said putting my hand on my forehead as the walls started to spin.

"You don't handle shit nigga, all that sound good but I see the real bitch in you," Julian said.

"Both y'all nigga shut the fuck up! My damn child look like she about to pass out and y'all wanna have a who's got the biggest dick contest," my father said as my eyes rolled into the back of my head.

"Shit that ain't a contest, but I'm out," Julian said again walking towards the front door.

"I'm following y'all asses to the hospital," Uncle Bo said.

"Nigga you not thinking clearly how they fuck you gone explain how everybody got shot? Hit Emily and doc and tell them meet us at the trap," I heard my father say before the door closed behind us. Julian limped out to the car, opened the door and placed me on the front seat. I felt him putting my seat belt on just before everything around me faded black.

****

BEEP! BEEP!

As my eyes fluttered open, I looked around confused for a second on where exactly I was at. It took me a few minutes to recall the last things I remembered. I tried sitting up as I looked around and noticed Julian walking into the room hanging up his phone.

"Stop trying to sit up," he said in annoyance.

"Why did I end up in the hospital? How long was I out? Is the baby ok?" I asked firing off question after question.

"You've been out about three hours. We got here around 7:30 and it's almost midnight now," he said as I placed my hand over my now bandaged head.

"My head is killing me," I groaned again trying to sit up.

"Stop trying to sit up. Man yo ass is hardheaded and don't listen for shit which gone be a problem the more you are around me. I don't fucking like to keep repeating myself. As a matter of fact ain't nobody around me that I repeat myself with but your ass and my patience running real fucking thin doing it," Julian said running his hands through his dreads.

"If you would answer at least one of my questions, you wouldn't have to repeat yourself. How is my baby?" I asked again rubbing my hands over my stomach.

Usually I felt movement, but at the moment, I didn't feel a thing.

"Oh my God I can't feel my baby moving!"

"Everything was checked out bruh my son is fine," he said.

"But my baby isn't moving! Why isn't my baby moving Julian!"

"Listen, the pigs been coming in here for the past hour, I just saw them walking back down the hallway. They ass not going away so we need to get some shit straight real quick. The story is you was robbed, attacked and I came home just as the robbers were fleeing the scene and got shot in the leg," He said not bothering to answer one of my questions.

"But what's going on with my baby?" I asked panicking as I felt tears running down my face.

"Damn Gabriela, nothing is wrong with the baby shawty, you need to tighten up this shit serious. If you gone be with a nigga," he was saying just as my room door opened again and this time two men in suits came in as one brandished his badge. Quickly wiping my tears, I tried to get my composure under control as one of them started talking.

"Hello Ms. Walters, I'm Detective Johnson and this is Detective Galloway. We are assigned to your case. Now, can you tell us in your own words what happened that led to your home being burglarized and shot up?" He asked me.

I looked from him, to his partner, to Julian who walked over to me and rubbed my belly. A few minutes ago when I touched my stomach, my baby didn't budge an inch, but the second Julian touched me, the little brat went to kicking up a storm. I was slightly jealous but also relieved and happy all at the same time.

"See I told you," Julian said to me.

His tone had softened up a bit and I didn't know if it was because of the detectives being in the room with us or not. I leaned my head on his shoulders as the feeling of him rubbing my belly and my baby stomping on my bladder soothed me.

"Miss Walters, if we could have a minute of your time," one of the detectives started to say before Julian cut him off,

"With all due respect, she and my child have already both been through a lot tonight, all she needs to do right now is rest. Can't you see she not doing so well? Why can't this wait until she is discharged?" Julian said sounding so professional.

"We understand that and we won't take up too much of her time, this is standard procedure given the fact that multiple gun shots were reported and the severity of the matter. Although no fatalities were reported, as of yet, that is something we want to prevent before it happens. All we need Miss Walters to do is fill in a few missing gaps for us about what happened," the detective said. Now that I knew my baby was ok, I felt back in my element as I sprang into action. I might not have shined in what I was slowly realizing was Julian's crazy world, but this, this was my world.

"I honestly can't even begin to describe what happened because everything happened so fast. I had just gotten home, I came in, I closed the door but I'm not even sure if I locked it behind me or not. I reside in a pretty decent neighbor where crime is practically none existent. I wasn't feeling good and needed to lay down because I am pregnant and already slightly high risk as it is. I was so exhausted that I didn't make it any further than the living room couch which was where I went to lay down at. A few minutes into my nap was when I discovered intruders in my home. I keep all my case files at home now and am responsible for countless criminals being put away. Some without the possibility of parole if they didn't have what was in my files such as witness statements and such," I said.

"Why did they specifically target you and no one else at the firm? Did you receive any threats prior to this attack? And you just happen to keep this Information just laying around your home?" The detective said.

"No I did not receive any prior threats, and everyone is assigned to different cases based on their levels of experience and success rate. Unfortunately, all crazy cases such as the ones I typically deal with tend to fall on my desk. And, normally I would keep files in my office, but I recently left the company to open my own practice, so I had no choice but to store them at my home," I said.

"And someone just happened to know you quit?" He said.

"They could if they are attached and or involved in a case I was working on. Ethically I am required to inform all of my clients of my departure, and of course opposing attorneys from cases that were in the appeal stage. Naturally one wouldn't assume I would have files at home, that was just by sheer luck they happened to guess right," I said answering every question he threw out at me confidently not missing a beat at all.

"Your home is very nice, especially for a young up and coming lawyer's salary."

"My home was a gift from my father Carlos Walters, I'm sure you've heard of him from all the successful million dollar business throughout Georgia," I said.

Even though I had bought my house with majority of my own money because my income was very good, he didn't need to know that. I wasn't offering any more information than I had to.

"Well," he started again before I cut him off because I was done with this game.

"Gentleman I have answered every question I've been asked to the best of my ability. This conversation seems to be turning from generic questions to interrogations, which is crossing all lines. If you have any more questions pertaining to the robbery and attempted murder of me and my child, you can contact me at this number," I said reaching over to the desk grabbing a pen and quickly jotting my business line down before handing it to them.

That let them know I was ending the free talk, and I didn't have to say contact my attorney because it was understood I would represent myself if need be.
"If we have any more questions, we will give you a call thank you for your time," Detective Galloway said as he and his partner offered us a fake smile, and exited the room.

I waited a few minutes after they were gone before finally speaking up.
"What was that back at the house with my uncle Julian?"
"The less you know, the better," he said tossing my phone on my bed before turning and walking back out the room. What the hell did that mean?

****

"I brought you some pajamas clothes so you can get out of this horrible hospital gown," my step mother said.

When Julian left, I didn't have long to process everything that he had just told me or the conversation with the detectives because my mother came into my room a few minutes later.

"Thank you, where is daddy?"

"He'll be in shortly; he received a business call that he had the take. How you feeling baby?"

"Other than this headache, I'm ok," I said looking towards the door half expecting Julian to come back in. I wanted him to explain what was going on.

No scratch that, I needed him to break dish every detail and explain the events that occurred in my house to me. Not only did I need to know for myself why my child's father, and possibly my boyfriend harmed my uncle because I had no idea they even knew each other. I also legally needed to know the situation so I could be fully prepared for those detectives and equipped to deal with any surprises they tried to throw my way. Something told me this wouldn't be a quick open and closed case judging by their line of questioning.

"I'm surprised I beat your friends here, especially Stacy," she said.

"She's in jail until Monday," I said half listening to her as I picked up my phone sending Julian a quick message.

"Jail? With Stacy I'm not surprised, she's a wild one at times."

"She is but she isn't totally wrong this time, and technically I'm the reason why she's in there," I said as I also sent a quick text to Destiny who quickly replied back.

"You're the reason, how? Talk to me Gabs, I feel like I don't even know you anymore. We used to talk about any and everything. Your first period, your first kiss, and even when you lost your virginity, but this pregnancy you keep from me? Not only did you keep the pregnancy a secret for so long, you never even mentioned dating someone new," my step mother said as I put my head down in shame.

It felt like I was disappointing everyone. Looking up, I noticed her eyes bore the same look of sadness and disappointment in them as my father and uncle.
"I didn't intentionally keep the pregnancy a secret from everyone, I just didn't know how to process it myself, let alone explain it to anyone else. How could I explain I was pregnant by a man who I wasn't dating, and didn't even know lived in the United States I met Julian in Jamaica and he was just different, intriguing," I said with a smile as I recalled our first meeting each other. I had bodily had sex with a stranger whose name I didn't even know, in a random person's office that night. Even though I was so out of my element, I felt so vibrant, alive and free that entire trip. The feeling I have with Julian is a feeling I want to experience for the rest of my life. I know it's too early to

be rushing back into a situation, and having a baby isn't a valid reason to be with him. But, the way my body, mind and soul craved Julian was a feeling I couldn't explain.

"You love him don't you baby?" My step mom said snapping me out of my thoughts. I didn't even realize I had tuned our entire conversation out.

"I don't know, maybe," I said glancing towards the door again.

"Judging by how many times you've looked at that door, I know you love him," she said.

"Huh?"

"You not looking for your father continuously looking at that door. You looking for your man," she said calling me out on my shit. When I didn't say anything, she continued talking,

"I see that glow in your face, and how your eyes lit up when I mentioned you spoke about him. I'm glad you finally moved on from that asshole Chance, this happy glow looks good on you. But trust me when I tell you a lot comes with loving a man like him. A lot that you were not exposed to, and was shielded from growing up. I made sure of that, even when me and your father were just on dating terms, back when he still wanted to run around town sleeping with everything wearing a skirt, I made sure you didn't witness anything you didn't need to see," she said which was news to me because that's not how I remember my childhood.

"What do you mean a man like that?"

"A man," she was saying until the door opened and my eyes slid to it eagerly thinking it was Julian, but it was just my father who I was also equally excited to see though. He walked in looking like nothing had happened to him at all. Matter of fact, if I wasn't there to witness it with my own eyes, I would swear he hadn't been hurt at all. I opened my mouth to comment on it but he held his hand up silencing me. He simply opened the jacket of the sweat suit he was wearing pulling it down a bit revealing the neatly dressed up on his arm. Even though I knew he was ok, the reality of what happened suddenly hit me hard. My father could have lost his life today, and for what? I'm the one that had called them over, so it felt like this was my fault. I really could have lost the only biological parent that I have left. That reality caused tears to instantly spring to my eyes. My father walked over and grabbed me into his arms before saying,

"Don't cry my Rose, I'm ok, this shit just a scratch," he said.

"It's all my fault."

"Hell no. It's them niggas fault for doing that shit in front of you. They could have handled that shit in the streets," he said. Pulling away from him, I said,
"What happened that's so bad daddy? Like why they do that to each other?"

"You gone have to ask your Uncle Bo or that fuck nigga that because that's their business. You are my business and my only concern. I will say this though, after talking to your uncle getting the real story of what that nigga did, I definitely know I don't want you dealing with somebody like Legend. That's not the type of man I wanted for my baby girl. Hell I would have chosen Chance over his ass because he makes that nigga look like a saint. But, seeing how he handled you today, a blind fool can see he loves you," he said.

"You don't know the man I know; Julian isn't like that."

"Listen baby, I'm not ashamed that I made the decision to let you choose to believe the world was sugar and spices and everything nice. You my daughter, I always want you to see the good out of life, and that's probably my one mistake as a parent. I know I gave you a hard time about Chance and for good reason but listen to me Gabriela, the person you see is not the person that that nigga is. You see Julian because you want to see "Julian." What happened at your house doesn't even scratch the surface with what that nigga Legend is capable of," he said his words sending a cold chill down my body.

Hearing my father speak this way about Julian sent my mind into overdrive. Whatever he did to my uncle had to have been serious enough for both of them to want to kill each other. And, from the sounds of it, it's not more so what my uncle did, but what Julian did to him. Was my father right? Did I block all the bad in people out of my mind because I wanted to see the good in them? I did know what type of person Chance was but I simply decided to try harder in my relationship instead of walking away. Was I prepared to deal with the truth behind this feud? And the real question is, after finding out the truth could I really move past all of this and still chose to be with a man like Legend?

LEGEND

"**Y**o I'm telling yo ass, the way she handled herself in there with them damn pigs, shawty a beast real talk. She went from crying to bossing up on their asses," I said taking a pull of my blunt handling it back to Cream. I had already heard Gabriela was a beast in the court room, but to see her ass tighten up that fast and be on point with them detectives was impressive as hell. If it were a better time, I would definitely ask her to look into my brothers case, but I couldn't think about that at this exact moment when I had my own shit storm to deal with. He still was a main and top priority of mines as well though.

"Shit even though that bullshit ass lawyer you got on retainer ain't doing much of shit for Case and I'll end up popping his ass soon, so bro gone need another one; I still don't know about letting her look into anything just yet. I mean look at all this shit we just found out about her. You trust her ass that much L? Shit you just told me Silas the nigga we been looking for, the nigga that tryna affect the way u feed myself, that bitch nigga is her damn uncle. Real or pretend it don't fucking matter because that shit suspect as fuck to me," Cream said taking a few pulls of the blunt handing it back to me.

I took it from him taking long ass pulls from it as I put my head back on the seat letting what he just said marinate in my mind as I allowed the weed to flood my systems and do its job. We were sitting in his car in a parking lot across the street from the hospital. I had called him to meet me here after I left Gabriela's house.

"Malechi ass getting cancelled soon make no mistake about it. That bitch ass nigga wasn't even trying to get Case a bond, but he damn sure accepted my payment already. I really felt like he trying me like his ass except from catching a bullet because he a damn lawyer. He obviously didn't thoroughly do his fuckin research on me because I would pop a judge if the nigga tried me and worry about the consequences later. Ain't nan nigga walking this earth gone play with me and like a man ima stand on that shit every time," I said meaning every word of that shit. If my pops and big brother didn't teach me shit else, they taught me to stand on all ten toes and never let a nigga play with you.

Shit that's why my brother went down fighting when they tried to jack him instead of just giving them niggas the drugs, he damn sure made them work for it. Took three of them niggas to the grave with his ass and pops damn sure took a few cops down before they finally got his ass into custody. I might be more calculated than them niggas and moved smarter, but I was still prepared to die about my respect. How Malechi was dragging his feet with this issue let me know he damn sure didn't respect me because if he had, he would have made a breakthrough, got a bond, or something. Anything other than constantly telling me it was nothing he could do. I continued talking as I said,

"Silas being her uncle doesn't change shit on my end, I'm still bodying that nigga. He's done too much to keep his life, the nigga tried to get at my momma today, and cost me money when he ran in my traps. Bottom line is you know I don't give a fuck about no family," I said.

"Do you trust her ass though because you never answered that shit? Cuz if you put that nigga to sleep, who is to say she won't run her mouth to them pigs? That shit would cripple us because we already lost Case, your team can't lose you. This how niggas eat! I know you don't want to admit it out loud, but I know yo ass and you fuck with shawty harder than you wanna admit. But, no face no case, so regardless of her being your seed's mother, you may have to put her ass down with that nigga. You prepared for that?" Cream asked me.

I knew this question was coming, and although I thought I was prepared for it, my heartbeat strangely began to speed up as my chest became tight just at the mere thought of the shit which blew me. Never in my life had I cared about another woman this much other than my mom's. When Gabriela told me her Uncle Bo was really Silas, my ears had heard her ass, but my brain was like fuck that bitch she can die with these muthafuckas. However, when I pulled that trigger, I made sure to hit anything but her ass. That had to be what this love shit was about right? Cuz no matter what lie I wanted to tell myself, I knew for a fact Gabriela made me feel shit I couldn't explain. The moment I found out the dates when she got pregnant lined up with the time she was with me in Jamaica, everything changed. I already was feeling shit for her before, but to know she was carrying my seed, was a completely different feeling altogether. One that would make me lay a nigga down on sight at the mere thought of her getting hurt. Still, I didn't like being knocked off my square like being around her clearly was doing.

"Nigga it's taking you a long ass time to answer the question which should tell you something. If you don't think you can body shawty yourself, just say the word and I got you. I'll make it quick and as painless as possible out of respect," Cream said snapping me out of my thoughts.

"My nigga different blood flows through our veins, and although yo ass white and I'm Jamaican, that doesn't mean shit to me. You still my brother and can't no nigga walking this earth tell me differently. I'll take a bullet for yo ass real shit. But you too damn eager to pop Gabriela and that shit got my trigger finger itching, and you know how I get when that shit happens. Just like I'll take a bullet for you cuz you my brother, that's my child's mother whom I'll pop yo ass over," I said without a trace of laughter and a serious look on my face letting his ass know I meant business.

I knew I was going against every rule I always told him and Case about. Don't fall in love with the pussy and get blindsided, never trust these hoes, and it's always bro's before hoes. But shit with Gabriela was just different even though I couldn't fully understand my feelings, I knew I would kill anything moving about her ass, and I do mean anything.

"Nigga ima let that shit slide because you obviously in your lit feelings right now, but you know me and you know I'm with all the same shit you with my nigga. Shit I'm just trying to look out for your ass cuz it's obvious you not thinking straight right now. The Legend I know wouldn't even be moving like this or contemplating whether or not to put a bitch down who potentially poses a threat to everything he's worked his ass off for. Especially not no bitch who fucking with the enemy, that's automatic grounded to get popped! You play chess with these niggas not checkers, you think everything through before it happens and make sure you thoroughly know a fucking person. Yet, you never bothered to look into Gabriela after you found out she was in fact your baby momma. Had you had Tan look into the shit, maybe Silas bitch ass would have come up somewhere in that search. A picture at a dance recital, graduation, law school, shit something. Look what fucking with this bitch done got you, shot the fuck up. When was the last time your ass even got shot? Shit not once in these past few years, yet you sitting in my car with bloody clothes getting that shit all over my custom peanut butter seats which you buying me a new Benz by the way. And, you still ain't answered my damn question, "Cream said laying into my ass.

Everything he had said to me was true as fuck, and if your homie, your brother couldn't put you in your place or correct you when you're wrong, then that ain't your brother. Still I wouldn't be me if I sat back and let his ass talk to me like that though right or wrong. I didn't even respond to him as I put the blunt out and got out of the car closing the door. However, instead of limping back across the parking lot to the hospital, I instead walked around to his side of the car just as he was getting out as well. Without saying a word, I instantly caught his ass with a mean ass right hook to his face as he countered back with a jab of his own on the side of my head and we both started swinging on each other going blow for blow neither one of us willing to back down. Cream wasn't scared to fight, the nigga just wasn't much of a fighter, he was more of the nigga you called if you wanted a nigga to disappear without a trace. Still, my nigga had heart no matter what which I respected the most about his ass. After a few minutes, we both found ourselves tired as hell as I pushed him off of me breathing hard as hell. This was the second fight my ass had had today and my body was mad as fuck with me about the shit. My leg was also starting to throb as I looked down noticing I was bleeding again meaning I had probably torn my damn stitches. We both looked at each other with a mean mug, as I walked up on his ass again with a frown on my face. After a few minutes, both our stupid asses burst out laughing as we dapped each other up pulling each other into a brotherly hug. Neither one of our dumb asses thought it was shit wrong with what we just did.

"You ain't have to hit me in my face ole ugly ass nigga. You just jealous cuz I look better than you. That ain't gone stop shit though cuz them hoes still gone be boppin on a nigga dick, that's why you mad huh?" Cream said laughing.

"Nigga I ain't fucked up about them weak ass hoes you be hittin, you know my dick ain't missing shit," I said laughing as he pulled another blunt out sparking that shit up hitting it a few times before passing it to me. My leg was killing me at this point, but I sucked that shit up as I took the blunt and leaned against his car as I took a few pulls from it.

"To answer your question, I don't know how she gone look at me after I kill this nigga, but I do trust her little ass with my life. Do I think she'll rat my ass out? I don't because her stubborn ass didn't have to let me take her to the hospital, trust me had she not wanted to go her pops damn sure would have let me take her ass out that house. With both her pops and Silas bitch ass bleeding, she still put her faith in my ass. You didn't see what I saw how she handled herself with them detectives either. Hell she didn't even look twice at their card when they gave it to her. If she had, that would have let me know she had thoughts of doubling back and calling their assess. You know I don't lay my head at muthafuckas crib, but I sleep comfortably at her shit as well. But you right, I'm slipping bad bruh, this is why I be on some fuck love type shit. Bitches will knock you off your square and have you fucking up. I been so caught up in trying to get Case out, trying to find Silas, trying to get a new connect, running this empire again, and trying to protect Gabriela and my seed, and keep them safe," I said This shit was crazy as hell because on one hand I loved the fuck out of Gabriela, but on the other hand I felt like maybe I had to distance myself from her to fully get my head on track. Because, who's to say I wouldn't lose my life the next time I let love blind my dumb ass and I get caught slipping again. I passed the blunt back to Cream as he took a long pull from it before coughing and saying,

"Naw you ain't tripping son, yo ugly ass just in love. I never thought I would see the day. Shit you liked Myriah but you love shawty in there. It's cool, I get it, well I don't cuz it's fuck love get money on my end. But you my brother and if you say she cool, then sis cool I can respect that and you know as long as I'm breathing ima give her the same loyalty I give you and my brother Case," Cream and I've known him long enough to know he meant that shit.

"You know I appreciate that shit," I said.

"Yeah yeah whatever ugly ass nigga let me get this bag of clothes you asked me to bring so you can let them fix them damn stitches and get out them bloody ass clothes. If they ask why you came back inside fucked up, just say a crackhead tried to rob you in the parking lot," his ass said laughing as he popped his trunk.

We joked around outside for a few more minutes before I walked back inside the hospital and got them to fix my stitches before I washed up, changed clothes and headed back to Gabriela's room to check on her and my child.

*****

"I still haven't found a way to get a passport on such short notice for someone who has never had one," Tan said to me.

She had called me early this morning walking me up out of my sleep to tell me she still wasn't having any luck getting my momma a passport from Jamaica to the United States.

"Didn't I fucking tell you it wasn't a price tag on the shit? You telling me it's no way to expedite the application at all?" I barked.

I wasn't as mad at her as I was at my own self for not taking care of shit like this sooner. But I never thought moving moms was an issue because nobody really knew where she stayed at in Jamaica, and the ones on the island who knew, also knew how ruthless I was and would rather chop their own leg off than to harm her. I don't know how Silas found her, but I guess if I could find his mother, he damn sure could find mines. I know what comes with this shit so all I can do is make sure she safe before I end this war before it even gets started.

"Look Legend, I haven't gotten any sleep because I've been up all night trying to exhaust every resource I have. I've turned over each stone that I could, I'm good at what I do, but it's limits to even what I can do," she said. I knew she was doing everything that she could do so I wasn't mad at her.

"Bet, listen rent me a jet for the weekend, make sure all the shit legit but put it in somebody else name, I don't want any traces of me ever being on this jet to surface," I said as the wheels in my head started turning.

I tried to do shit the legal way, now it was time to do what I did best. If I couldn't get my mother here with me with permission, I was about to simply grant my damn self permission because I was about to do shit Legend's way.

"Ok anything else?" Tan asked.

"Make sure it's fully equipped with extra cargo space and a casket," I said.
"A casket?"

"No questions Tan just make it happen. Oh, and you've earned a bonus that you'll be receiving today. Never think the shit you do for a nigga goes unnoticed," I said to her before hanging up.

I may be an asshole but like I said I made sure my entire team was eating because contrary to some niggas beliefs, you are only as strong as your team is. So, I made sure all my niggas were eating steak and lobster dinners even after I retired. If they were eating noodles right now, that's what they earned, ain't shit in this business free everybody carried their own weight. After I got off the phone with Tan, I called my momma. I glanced over to Gabriela's bed where she was knocked out snoring with her mom wide open as I smiled to myself while shaking my head at her ass. As pretty as she was, her ass sounded like a bear when she was sleep. The doctors had cleared her pending her lab results coming back fine. They already confirmed her and the baby were fine, they just needed to take it easy the next couple weeks.
"Hail?" (Hello) my mother said when she finally answered the phone.

"Wah mek it tek yuh suh lang tuh ansah di phone muma?" Why it took you so long to answer the phone ma?)

"Blurtnawt yuh mean it tek mi suh damn long! laas time mi check mi did yuh damn mada Julian yuh did nuh mines! Watch yuh mout before yuh lose yuh tung" (What you mean it took me so damn long! Last time I checked I was your damn mother Julian you were not mines! Watch your mouth before you lose your tongue) she shot back at me. If people thought black

CAUGHT UP IN A DOPEBOY' LOVE 2

woman were crazy, they haven't seen shit yet until they've met a Jamaican woman. No matter how old they are, all their asses crazy!

"Calm dung ma mi apologize yuh kno wah mi mean Shit crazy right now mi need yuh tuh ansah soon as mi call,"(Calm down ma I apologize, you know what I mean. Shit crazy right now I need you to answer soon as I call.)

"Yuh don't haffi remind mi what's gwaan mi bloodclot yaad burn dung mi kno exactly wah di hell gwaan I'm still yuh mada Julian Santiago Jr,"(You don't have to remind me what's going on, my bloodclot house burned down I know exactly what the hell going on I'm still your mother Julian Santiago Jr) she said.

I let her go off on my ass for a few more minutes before I had her put Kojo, one of the men on my payroll watching over her on the phone.

"Wah Gwaan," Kojo said.

"What's going on that way?" I asked him skipping the pleasantries getting straight to business.

"Everything everything pan fi wi end We've been keeping fi wi ears tuh di streets but it been silent wi haven't had any problems here at di hotel eitha."(Everything is everything on our end. We've been keeping our ears to the streets but it's been silent. We haven't had any problems here at the hotel either.)

"Bet, y'all hold tight, I'm coming for her real soon so stay sharp until then. I got eyes on the nigga who tried to get at her, but I know his ass didn't do it himself, he paid somebody down there. Now that he know she's not dead, I bet he gone try again, but he was sloppy the last time so this time you and your men better make sure none of the niggas who come that way leave breathing," I said.

"Truss mi brethren nuhting cum dis way mi queng di wull a

40

dem,"(trust me brethren if anything come my way I'll kill all of them)

That's all the confirmation I needed to hear. I hung the phone up as I noticed Gabriela waking up. When saw me, she started to sit up as I said,

"Take it easy."

"I'm fine Julian, quit treating me like a damn child," she snapped with an attitude.

Ever since I refused to tell her ass what the beef was with me and Silas, her ass done had this damn attitude. I knew I couldn't keep it from her forever, I just needed a little more time to kill his ass first, then I would pick and choose the parts I wanted to share with her. I wasn't like these other niggas who laid up and pillow talked with their woman about this street shit. Naw, I didn't want her involved in this lifestyle at all.

"Shawty lose the attitude though. You hungry?"

"I can get my own food, I don't need shit from you but the truth Legend," she said leaning over and paging the nurse.
"Oh now I'm Legend huh?" I smirked to keep from getting angry I wanted to choke her little ass, but I had actually read about how pregnant women got emotional, so I was gone chalk this shit up to that.

"Listen, I get that you mad and you feel like you left in the dark on this situation, but what your spoiled ass needs to get out your head is I'm not that fuck boy you was engaged to. That shit not gone fly with me so you need to check that fly ass mouth of yours," I said just as a nurse knocked before opening the door.

"Hey Ms. Walters, you needs anything?" She said.

"Yes, can somebody bring me something to eat? And do you know when I'll be discharged because I feel fine and I'm ready to get in my own bed," she said.

"Umm let's see," the nurse said looking down at the chart she had in her hands. "It seems your lab work came back and everything was fine. I will send the doctor in here shortly to discuss medicine he's prescribing you with while I start on your discharge paperwork."

"But how long will that take?" Gabriela impatiently asked.

"It shouldn't take long. I can't give you a definite time, but it will most definitely be sometime today. Someone will be back in with a food tray shortly in the meantime ok?" The nurse said as she turned and looked me up and down licking her lips discreetly as she brushed past me making sure to rub her body on mines as she passed by me.

"Listen, I have to go out the country tonight but I plan on being back tomorrow, Monday at the latest. So, when they discharge you, ima arrange for you to go to my place. It's secluded, and secure. Ima make sure you have a nurse and around the clock security-" I was saying until she cut me off.

"No I told my parents I was coming to their house until I found yet another place to live."

"Naw that don't work for my shawty, I need a status update on how you and my child doing every hour, and I can't get that at your parents' house. Besides, I don't want you anywhere near that nigga Silas," I said.

I didn't trust his ass, and still wasn't convinced he wasn't talking about Gabriela when he said he would kill everyone I loved and never got a chance to love. It was only pure coincidence I ran into her at that restaurant. Who is to say I would have ever known about the baby? I ain't fooled by this game his ass playing.

"What! That's my damn uncle! He's been there for me my entire life. It takes a village to raise a child and he definitely was a part of that village. It doesn't matter what you two have going on, that's still my uncle, and my godfather. You are the only outsider I don't really know," she said.

"Outsider huh? You don't really know me like that but that ain't once stopped you from choking on this dick. You wanna side with your people cool, choose the right side though Gabriela. In the meantime, long as you carrying my child you not going anywhere near that nigga! This not a debate, and I'm not about to argue with your ass because you already saw how I get when I feel played. About my child, nobody will be exempt. You keep trying me and I keep telling your ass you might want to play this childish ass game with somebody else," I barked.

I don't know what happened with her and her peoples, but she ain't been the same since I saw them coming out of her room. I hated to talk to her ass like this but I meant every fucking word I said. Her little feisty ass had the nerve to look me dead in my eyes before saying,

"Nobody is arguing with you, I'm telling you I'm not going to a house with people I don't know. I'm staying at my parents' house! You can try and take me to your house, but I guarantee you if I tell my father to come and get me he will!" She said which I had no doubt was true.

That nigga loved the fuck out of her ass which he should and I respected that because she was his child. I would feel the same way about my kid. I knew it was no arguing with her ass, and I damn sure didn't need her pops coming to my shit because his loyalty wasn't to me, it was to Silas. So, wasn't shit stopping him from telling that fuck nigga where I lived then I would have to kill her pops and her uncle.

"I'll be back in two days tops, so don't get comfortable because you coming with me," I said.

"You plan on telling me the truth in two days?"

"No," I said.

"Well I'll be at my father's house until you change your mind," she stubbornly said as I looked down at an incoming message on my phone.

"Two days Gabriela, and for your sake, don't make me come get you," I said texting away on my phone as I walked out of her room. I would feel better with her at my crib so my men could watch her, but after meeting her pops, I knew that nigga would die before something happened to her. Still, I wasn't trusting a soul with my seed but me, so I was serious when I told her ass don't unpack and get comfortable.

****

"So you sure the ice won't freeze her or anything?" I asked the niggas putting the ice inside of compartments they had built in under two hours in the casket.

"No, she will be perfectly fine inside of it. The ice will only act as means to lower the thermal reading on the casket when custom scans it. As humans we have a warmer body temperature that the dead do not have. So, when they scan the casket, if it reads anything above cold, they will know something is wrong. This will clear customs easily," Josh said adding two more bags of ice to the compartments.

Him and his brother were a part of my cleanup crew I always called to dispose of bodies for me. Since my mother's house had burned down and a body was found but couldn't be identified because of how badly it was burned, I planned to walk her as right through customs in that casket. Well not me personally but the pall bearers I hired which happened to just be Cream and Jaxson. I had a bitch who worked at the airport hook me up with a badge and an airport rank agent's orange vest. So, when the plane lands back in the States, as they getting the casket out, ima slip my vest on and slip through the airport undetected.

"What even gave your ass an idea to do some shit like this?"

Cream asked me.

His ass thought I was crazy when I ran the idea by him earlier. Now granted, I didn't know about the ice and all of that, but I thought about the casket because of the fire. Of course it made the news on the island because everyone knows who my father. His name still holds weight even after all of these years.

"Shit I don't know, it just came to me," I said watching the cameras I had put in Gabriela's hospital room.

Even though she still wasn't discharged when I left, when she went to the bathroom, I slipped a camera in her room so that I could monitor her for a few hours. If I thought I could successfully have a crew bug her people's house I would have. Even with how the fuck her ass talked to me, I still wanted to make sure she was ok. I may have lied to myself early and says I was only concerned about my seed, but shit that was a lie. Gabriela was just as much a priority to me even though she was mad at me. I had men posted all around the hospital, and some was even gone tail her ass when she left.

"And if this don't work?" Cream said jarring me out of my thoughts.

"I already got that covered as well, you know this," I said feeling like my old self again. I was just glad to be back k thinking clearer.

Once Josh was finished, I paid him as Cream helped him stash the coffin inside of one of the many secret compartments on the jet. He slipped off the plane making his way off the private airstrip as we all got comfortable preparing to take this flight to Jamaica. I wish we could slip back in using this same airstrip, because it would make my life and everyone else's so much easier. When I had a good day, everybody had a good day.

After I pulled my iPad out of my bag paying all of my employees for the week, as well as paying Tan a little bit extra, I found myself looking at baby shit on line for my lil nigga. I had found out the sex when they did an emergency ultrasound when Gabriela first made it to the hospital. The thought of a mini me terrorizing these streets both excused my ass, and somewhat worried me. I wanted more did my son than how I had to get it out the mud. But at the same time, my struggle and hustle is what molded me into the man I am today. I don't want to find myself making the same mistakes with my seed that I made with Case. I gave that nigga everything he ever asked for since he was old enough to talk, and look at him now? Barely legal drinking age in America and facing football numbers in jail.

"You know Stacy's ass went to jail yesterday for fuckin the other homegirl Chanel up," Cream said sitting down beside me.

"Good I never liked Chanel's ass. I thought about paying some hoes from around the way to get on her ass. I knew she had all that mouth for no reason," I said because I've told Gabriela numerous of times that I didn't trust that sneaky bitch.

"Apparently she was sleeping with Gabriela's ex fiancé the whole time," Cream said.

"Word? Damn shawty wasn't doing it like that was she? Wait nigga how the fuck you know this?"
"Shit her crazy ass told me when she called me. Apparently she can't get a bail until Monday. She locked up and all her ass was talking about was fighting shawty again when she gets out."

"Yo I believe her ass to. Stacy a real one. Remember she almost beat yo ass with that bat," I said laughing.

"Man on God I almost put her ass to sleep that night."

"Wait, she called you? From jail? But you have the nerve to be clowning me about my baby momma."

"Naw it ain't even like that, I drop dick off in her ass every now and then but we damn sure ain't on nothing else but friends with benefits. Shit she too much for my ass, so dick is all I got for her," he said.

"You only giving her dick, but she called your ass from jail and nigga you knew it was a jail call, yet you still pressed 1 to accept it," I said catching him in his lie. He was just down my throat about not admit my feelings about Gabriela, but his ass was doing the same thing with Stacy's ass.

"Shit because she never calls my ass for shit, so I knew this had to been serious." He shrugged.

"But why you care when you just giving her dick and that's it?" I asked not willing to drop the subject.

"Like I said me and shawty cool. Shit I can match a blunt with her ass and get the skin sucked off my dick all at the same time. Baby girl got skills, but I know where you going with this and it damn sure ain't that. Shit she called and yelled through the phone answer it's important. She told me that Gabriela left in a hurry and hadn't been answering for her, and she ain't know your number to call you. Apparently the nigga baby momma beat the fuck out of Chanel before letting them know Chanel the real reason the wedding was called off or some shit."

"Damn! I knew that bitch wasn't shit when she put Gabriela up to do that bullshit ass medicine challenge. She almost got her dumb ass friend popped for trying me like that," I said getting mad all over again thinking about her ass texting me talking about she gone ride him crazy and I'll never have a clue.

I just knew I was about to pop up and lay everybody ass down in that fucking crib.

"Hell yeah, but shit the phone hung up before she could tell me who this fuck nigga is," Cream said.

"Hit me with that info when you get it," I said lost in thought. The very idea of a nigga walking this earth that's done fucked Gabriela didn't set well with me. Shit she said she only been with me and that nigga, so when he die I'll be the only one who'll know how good that pussy feels. That's how crazy she had my ass going, about to murk another nigga for the pussy.

****

"Everything all set?" I asked the caller getting confirmation before I hung up. We had just touched down in Jamaica at a private airfield, and I was more than ready to get off this damn plane and stretch my legs.
"Ok y'all, we gone head to the hotel, grab my momma, then come back here, and head home." I said walking to the back of the plane opening one of the compartments up.

If you didn't know what to look for, you would assume it wasn't anything in there but medical supplies. However, I pressed twice on the floor board of the compartment as it lifted up. Pulling the board off the floor, I reached in and started pulling out guns passing one to each of them as I grabbed two more. Kojo said it was silent on their end but shit I would rather be prepared than be caught in the crossfire without my tool on me.

"Damn nigga, that's some next level shit dawg! You a fuckin genius," Jaxon said making sure his gun was loaded. He ass was barely eighteen, and a nigga Case had put on, but he was solid and I fucked with the lil nigga.

"I won't even ask," Cream said shaking his head." Aye hand me another clip."

After we had everything we thought we needed, they stepped off the plane as Cream and Jaxson went climbed into the SUV that was waiting for us. I stayed behind to talk to my pilot and his crew.

"We got enough fuel to make it back home or you gotta fuel up again?" I asked him.

"We should be fine, I'll have the crew run diagnostics and make sure we all set to make the return trip home Mr. Santiago," he

said.

"I'll be gone two hours tops, have the engine warming up and already preparing for takeoff when we get back. I don't want us to stay on the ground a second longer than we have to Conner," I said.

"Rodger that" he said nodding at me. I walked down the ramp and opened the door getting into the backseat of the truck that Tan had arranged for us as I told him where we was going.

"Shit with Ma home, we bout to be eating good as hell," Cream said.

"Who is this we nigga?" I said laughing.

"Shit me and whoever else cop a plate of oxtails, rice and peas with fried plantain," his ass said.

"Hell yeah all that shit sound good" Jaxson said.

"It does and it's a Jamaica restaurant in "Atlanta that's sell all of that shit so that's exactly where you two ugly ass niggas gone be eating at," I said.

"Who? Shit that nigga might eat there but you and me both know Ma gone make sure I got a plate put up every time," Cream said which was true because ever since she first met Cream, she's embraced him and treated him like her own son.

She told me he looked like he needed a mother's love, so that's exactly what she gave him. That's just the type of person that she was and why it made it hard for anyone not to love her.
"Man I've never been to Jamaica, this shit lit. I gotta most definitely bring my shawty out this way," Jaxson said as we drove through the island.

"Yeah this shit dope, it ain't no place like it in the world," I said texting away on my phone.

"Aye once we grab ya moms, swing us by the hood, I wanna see the parts that was on Shottas," Jaxson said.

"Nigga this ain't no damn vacation, see that shit on yo own time. Besides, you ain't built for Kingston," I said as we pulled up to the hotel my mother was staying at.
I called Kojo up letting him know we were outside as I grabbed the duffel bag full of money I had grabbed off the jet and hopped out the truck to meet them.

"Wah Gwaan," Kojo said dapping me up when he saw me. I dapped him up then gave me the duffel bag as I glanced over his shoulder and noticed my mother smiling a little bit too damn hard in some young nigga face who was carrying her bags.

"Yo who that is?" I nodded my head behind him. He turned around to see who I was talking about just as I walked past him to where she was.

"That's just Drew him cool," Kojo said walking behind me.

"Fuck that nigga," I said walking up on them. I started to show my ass, but thought better of it.
"Wi haffi guh cum pan an get inna di cyar an get out dis nigga face." (We gotta go come on and get in the car and get out this nigga face) I said as I grabbed her by the arm. Shit I knew my pops was in jail doing his own thing hitting hoes left and right, but I had never seen my mother so much as look twice as another nigga. Yet here she was smiling in this nigga face showing all thirty two of her teeth and shit.
"Mi bredda mi mean no disrespect ya mon,"(My brother I meant no disrespect ya mon)Drew said throwing his hands up in surrender.

"Nonsense," my mother said waving me off as she told everyone bye and thanked them for everything they did for her as she walked ahead of me getting in the truck. I dapped Kojo up again as he said,

"Him honestly didn't mean nuhting by it yuh mada did cool shi cooked fi whulla wi an wen shi wasn't cursing wi out shi did lay back an chill."(He honestly didn't mean anything by it your mother was cool she cooked for all of us and when she wasn't cursing us out she was laid back and chill) Kojo said. I nodded my head but didn't say anything as I walked back to the truck and hopped in.

"Let's go," I said to the driver as I texted the pilot letting him know we were on our way back. We were about forty minutes from the airstrip.

"Ow a mi baby Julian mi wa fi chat tuh him."(How is my baby Julian I want to talk to him)

"That's nuh a damn baby mi kip telling yuh dat.(That's not a damn baby, I keep telling you that) I said to her as she reached over and popped me upside my head.

"Wah mi tell yuh bout dat mout."(What I tell you about that mouth) she said.

"Did this nigga just get a whopping?" Cream said laughing.

"Hell yeah," Jaxson said.

"Fuck both y'all niggas," I said as my mother raised her hands again to my ass.

"You better stop while you ahead," Cream joked.

"Yuh nuh need fi tell him nuhting him aready knows him can't chat tuh mi like dat wah mek yuh mad mi did thanking di nice man Julian?"(You do not need to tell him anything he already knows he can't talk to me like that. Why you mad I was thanking the nice man Julian?) she said.

"Because you don't need to be all in his face," I said not bothering to say it in patios. Her ass understood me she just liked to only speak Jamaican.

"Stella got her groove back why can't she?" Jaxson said but

even Cream shook his head no at him. Before I could reach over and smack the shit out of that nigga, a bullet flew through the driver's window splattering his brains all over the dash board and seat as we swerved into incoming traffic as my mother let out a loud piercing scream.

"Fuck," I said throwing my mother to the ground as I jumped up reaching over the seat grabbing the wheel a second before we were hit by another car.

As soon as I got control of the wheel, bullets rang out of nowhere flooding the truck as I climbed over the seat putting my feet on the pedal as I opened the door throwing the driver out of it. Shit he knew what came with taking this job, I would send money to his peoples later. Right now, my number one priority was getting my mother to safety, unharmed. I let something happen to her and pops would break out of jail and personally kill me his damn self.

"What the fuck yo!" Jaxson yelled letting his window down firing at the niggas who had pulled up on side of us in vans firing at us.

Since this was my home and I knew these streets like the back of my hand, I floored the truck getting off the main highway cutting through parking lots as Cream and Jaxson were hanging out their window laying niggas down.

"Gimme a gun I'll kill all dem bumbaclots"(Give me a gun I'll kill all them bumbaclots) my mother said. Back in the day before my father made her ass sit down, she used to be right beside him thuggin it out in them streets.

So, I knew she knew how to shoot a gun, still I damn sure wasn't about to have her out here in no damn shoot out. What that say about me as man to have my mother doing that?

"Hell Naw, don't pass her ass shit," I said pulling a gun out shooting out my side window as I stomped down on the gas pedal even more.

I wanted to get in on the action so badly, but neither Cream nor Jaxson's ass knew where to go and I damn sure wasn't gone put my mother in the driver's seat. Calm me crazy, but heart started racing and my adrenaline shot up because this type of shit I lived for right here.

"Man L you know where the fuck you going bruh?" Cream yelled.

"Yeah we almost their nigga get ready to move," I said making a sharp right crashing into the van that had swerved up on us causing them to flip over.

It was still at least four vans on our ass. Turning down a dirt road, Jaxson said,

"I'm out of bullets."

"I'm almost out," Cream said as I yelled,

"The backseat lets down, press the sides of the seats," I said.

"Nigga what we supposed to do hide in the trunk?" Cream said.

"Just open the shit nigga and shut the fuck up," I said.
The backseats led to the trunk where I had them packs guns and extra clips. Like I said, I didn't expect us to walk into a war, but I'm a nigga that's always prepare for whatever. I knew not to underestimate Silas ass no matter who much he said he didn't gun for my mother; I knew his ass did. What I didn't understand was why he waited until I came to get her to finish the job? This that bitch shit I be talking about. As the airstrip came into view, Cream and Jaxson were still firing at the cars as I saw more vans swerving up on them in my rear view mirror.
"These niggas keep coming out of nowhere," Jaxson said as I drove us up on the runway.

"Damn there go some more of them niggas up ahead. How we gone do this bruh? Fuck it if I gotta die, I'm going down fighting,"

Jaxson said saying that shit with not a quiver in his voice showing no signs of fear.

That's what I meant by the lil nigga being solid because most niggas his age would have been folded.

"Ok let's move," I said putting the car in park as the niggas in the vans ahead of us on the runway had started to get out of their van.

All of them were strapped with big ass guns as they advanced towards us. Some were right by the opening to get in the jet, while others had branched out a bit. We had niggas in front of us and niggas behind us.

"Shit I got your back," Cream started,

"Until that casket drop," I said. "Now cover my ma with this jacket and move," I yelled as I made sure I was locked and loaded before hopping out the front as they hopped out the back.

By this time the niggas in front of us had advanced on us. But, instead of them shooting at us, they started shooting at the niggas behind us as I turned around firing on their asses as well as Cream handed my mother off to Jaxson while he started firing as well. We were backing up shooting at the same time until we made it to the steps of the jet. By this time, it looked like a blood bath on that runway as bodies were laid out everywhere. Pulling the stairs up, I told the pilot to take off as I walked back to where everybody else was. Walking over to momma, I thoroughly examined her body checking all over for a bullet wound. With adrenaline racing, you could be shot and not even realize it because you so focused on something else.

"I'm fine bowy I'm fine,"(I'm fine boy I'm fine) she said swatting my hands away from her.

"Man who the fuck them niggas was who just saved our ass? I almost got to firing on their asses," Jaxson said?"

"I hit Kojo up before I got off the jet and told him to get some of his men together and have them head to the strip. I didn't know we would be coming in hot like that, but just in case them nigga dropped their nuts, I was prepared," I said.

That's why I dropped that duffel bag of cash off to him. Kojo though I was tripping when I told him to arrange for niggas to be there because he insisted it had been quiet this whole time. Shit they probably thought my mother's house being burnt down was an electrical issue at this point since the streets was quiet; but I knew better. If I wasn't the nigga I was and didn't think everything through, our asses would have been caught out here without guns and reinforcements and been pushing up dirt by now.

"Man this shit with Silas getting out of hand, now I'm pissed off because the nigga just played with my life. They all gotta see me fuck that," Cream said as Jaxson agreed.

"It's been out of hand since he made them empty threats, but yes see us they most definitely will," I said taking a seat as the wheels in my head begin to turn.

GABRIELA

"Bitch I need another drink for this shit," Destiny said.

We were currently at her house eating Juicy Crab as I filled her in on everything that had happened in my life in the last two days including what went down at my house.
After I finished telling her everything she was silent for a moment before speaking up.

"Listen, I figured your ass didn't know this, but since all this shit happened, it all makes sense now," Destiny said.

"What all makes sense now?"

"Well you know I be fucking with my lil' yeah and he push drugs. Well I overheard him talking Friday night about Legend making them all move into the traps since one of them got hit or some shit like that. But how he was going on and on about it, I gathered Legend gotta be the boss," she said.

"Boss of what?" I asked.

"Bitch I know you not that fucking slow, he the head nigga in charge of this street shit. You went from fucking with Chance the worker to Legend the boss," Destiny said dropping a bomb on me.

"Julian isn't a drug dealer, he's a business owner," I said.

"Shit he could be that as well, all big time drug dealers getting big money not chump change, have legal businesses. Trust me

I've fucked with enough to know that. Anyway, I'm sure whatever beef him and your uncle has, it has to be street related to make them two niggas wanna kill each other like that," Destiny said.

"My uncle is not a drug dealer, that I know for a fact. I've personally been to a few of his boring company parties when I was younger," I said.

"Shit he might not be dealing drugs directly, but he did something to make the street nigga in Legend come out. Why else would your uncle already have a gun if it was a simple misunderstanding?" She said which made sense because both of them had their guns drawn.
As a matter of fact right before Julian fired, he accused me of setting him up. Could my uncle really be involved in something illegal? I guess Julian isn't the only person I don't really know. All this was too much for me to deal with right now. I couldn't believe this was happening to me. I leave one man who was into drugs, just to fall in love and get pregnant but another one. Apparently I didn't know anything about Julian, but I was learning an awfully lot about Legend.

"Bitch stop looking like you lost your best fucking friend," Destiny said.
"How the hell do I keep falling for men like this Destiny?" I cried.

"Shit simple, you love them hood niggas. It's ok sis, we all do the hooder they are the better the sex is. Can't nobody fuck you better than a hood nigga," she said.

"Chance must not have a lick of hood in his ass then," I said shaking my head.

"Bitch you toe up, but shit he had something, had your ass gone. A hood nigga with a good mouth piece will talk a bitch out their clothes, their rent money, and their car," she said as I started laughing.

It's the first time I've really laughed since all of this went down.

"No seriously Destiny, what am I going to do? I can't deal with this, him standing on the corner doing drugs," I whined.

"Bitch please that nigga ain't standing on no damn corner, that a boss. Listen Gabriela, we all baby you. Me, Stacy, your family, and hell even that ugly bitch Chanel. You the baby of the group even though you not the youngest. We just know you not into the shit we are and that's ok. So it's places me and Stacy go by ourselves and don't even invite your ass and shit we do that's we don't tell you about. Like scan only two items at the self-check out in Walmart. You over react about everything instead of going with the flow," she said.

"Because I'm a lawyer! I took an oath and I happen to take that very seriously! I've worked my ass off to get to where I am! I overreact because it could cost me my license."

"Ok bitch chill that's not the damn point I'm getting at. The point I'm trying to make is you are shielded from shit by mostly everybody in your life for a reason. Show people you can handle the truth, and they'll tell it to you. Shit I been your best friend for years and even I know yo ass is difficult to talk to so imagine how other people feel. You need to stop all this crying and get your shit together. You constantly showing your weakness and that's why Chance always walked all over you, had a baby on you, and had you playing step momma while he still fucked around in these streets. That's why Chanel thought she could fuck your man then let you cry on her shoulders. The boss ass bitch you turn into when you step inside a court room is the person you need to be outside of court. No matter if you want to be or not, you tied to this nigga for life, so his problems are your problems. You gone boss up for your nigga? Or you gone keep crying and acting like a simple bitch, and let another street bitch come in and take your man. Cuz trust me if I got hold to a nigga like Legend I wouldn't give his ass back. Going by what

I seem him do for you, and what you just told me how he made sure you got to the hospital and didn't want you out of his sight. That's a street nigga's way of showing you that he loves you and he ride for you. You gone ride for him back?" She said putting me in my damn place.

She had also hurt my feelings and a part of me wanted to cry but I didn't want to see the look of disappointment in her eyes if I did.

"I don't know how to ride Destiny. Like how do I do that and not violate ethical rules of law? If Julian is into illegal activities, it directly ties me in them as well," I said.

"Not if you don't get caught bitch. Damn stop overthinking everything and put your big girl panties on. Just like you told me you handled them detectives, keep that same energy with Legend and maybe that nigga will start confiding in you. Shit right now you displaying weak bitch qualities, I wouldn't tell your ass shit either. Look how you just acted knowing I steal from Walmart from time to time. This nigga into bigger shit, shit that could land him in jail for life. Ain't nobody telling that shit to just anybody. You want him to be honest with you and trust you, start trusting his ass that shit work both ways. I've been dealing with hood niggas since I realized I was gay, and one thing they always told me they liked most about me was the fact that I was their peace. You always say I deserve better and stop being a secret, but I give niggas what they don't get from their baby mommas and girlfriends, I give them peace. That's all hood niggas want after they come in from risking their lives in the streets all day. Their dick sucked, a hot meal, and some peace. Shit how my lil yeah' was talking, it's getting hot in these streets so Legend definitely need some peace from your ass," she said giving me a lot to think about.

The more I replayed all my conversations with Julian in my head from when I first met him until he left me in the hospital to go out of town, the more I realized that maybe Destiny was right.

My father tried in so many words to tell me this as well, I just didn't comprehend it then. If my father knew Julian was a drug dealer, what did that mean for my father though? Destiny was right, everybody in my life shielded me from things like I was an invalid, but that shit stops today. I don't know I was gone do it, but I definitely was about to start getting truthful answers out of people.

****

"Lawd if you didn't come get my ass out of jail today I would have done some strange shit for a piece of change," Stacy said all dramatically as she hopped in the front seat. I had posted her bond as soon as they had given her one this morning, and she was finally getting released a few hours later.

"Like what? It's not like they have any money to offer you," I said pulling off.

"Shit they might not have any damn money, but they got food. A bitch ain't built for jail, that food nasty as hell. If I had to go one more day eating that mess, I was liable to buss my damn self out," she said all dramatically.

"That means you not going back then," I said.

"Oh naw because I definitely owe that hoe Chanel a proper ass whooping. Matter of fact I'm ready to go back, so ride me by that bitch house. Well naw I can't do no pull ups with your ass never mind. Me and Destiny can come back and put sugar in that hoe tank," Stacy said.

Normally I would just agree with her, but after my talk I had with Destiny yesterday with her telling me they treated me a certain way, I said,

"Put skittles in her tank that's more effective, and we have to wait a few days to do it. You just got out of jail for assaulting her, so your ass would definitely be the number one suspect to the crime. She not worth going back to jail over so we'll move smarter," I said as Stacy's mouth dropped open. Leaning over, she put her hand over my head,

"Bitch what's wrong with you? You feeling ok?"

"I'm fine stop being dramatic," I said pushing her hand off of me.

"Bitch you gotta be sick because you just told me how to commit a crime play by play. Not miss let me leave first before anything criminal happens," she said.

"Today's a new day, and I'm a new person." I said proudly.

"Bitch you been driving the speed limit since we left the jailhouse," she said laughing.

"I don't have to be driving like this grand theft auto and we running from the cops to be a different person. I'm just tired of people treating me differently, hell I didn't even realize how much it affected me until I was told that's what you all were doing," I said to her.

"Bitch what you talking about?" She asked me. I then told her everything Destiny had told me including everything that happened with Julian.

"Bitch I knew them niggas was drug dealers from day one when I met Cream's fine ass that night in the club. You know I can spot a hood nigga a mile away. Then when I started fucking with him, I picked up on all the signs. You didn't know that shit? Hell you was with Chance forever so how you didn't know how to spot a drug dealer?" she said.

"Chance never did any of that around me and never really talked about it," I said.

"That's because his ass wasn't doing shit worth talking about. Them lil ass nickel bags him and his crew was moving ain't shit compared to the level Legend and his crew on." Stacy said.

"How you know all this?"

"Shit you don't see your baby daddy? Does it look like he asking you for money here and there like Chance used to do? And shit every time Cream pull up on me his ass pushing a different car. Nobody gotta tell me shit, it's unspoken and understood them niggas some go getters and getting money on a different scale," she said.

I had noticed all the expensive things Julian had starting with his crazy huge house in Jamaica, but again that's because I thought he was a successful businessman.

"Is that why you chose Cream over Case?" I asked her.

I mean I knew she only liked Cream so much because he didn't like her, but now I'm thinking it was the line of work he was in.

"What you mean?"

"Well because Cream is a bad boy and Case isn't. He's just a wild party animal," I said.

"Bitch Case doing Fed time right now for the amount of drugs he was caught with. Shit he definitely far from a good boy. Case young ass sexy, but Cream just does something to my soul," she said.

"Wait, Case is in jail? Julian never told me this."

"Bitch you probably didn't give him a chance to. I found this out because Rhonda down at the swamp meat was talking about it with some bitch. Said ever since Case been in jail his side bitch been going around telling everybody she pregnant. The girlfriend eventually pulled up on her ass popped the trunk, pulled out a Louisville slugger and went to town on that hoe car. I asked Cream about him being in jail and he said yes but that's all he said. You would have thought I asked that nigga for some money how quick he cut that shit short," she said.

Damn so on top of everything Julian was dealing with, his

brother was also in jail! I knew how much Case meant to him, so I knew he was stressed out behind this.

"Wow! He really didn't trust me enough to confide in me any of this with me!" I said out loud but more so to myself.

"Bitch that nigga trust you more than you think, look at his actions. But then after you do that, go back and look at your actions back towards him. The only problem is you not him. But since my bitch say she bossing up on these hoes, keep that same energy when you see your nigga. Your actions gone speak louder than your words," she said giving me a lot to think about.

After I dropped her off, I headed to get some food before going back to my parents' house. Walking into the house, I headed into the kitchen to grab a bottle of water to go with my food. When I got in there, I heard my father talking in a heated discussion with someone who I assumed was my uncle from how the conversation was going.

"Either you gone pop the nigga or play these fuck games. This shit out of hand and I don't give a fuck what y'all got going on, my fucking child involved," my father said until he looked up and saw me standing there as he pressed end on the call.

Without saying another word, I pulled a chair out and sat down at the table.

"You didn't have to stop the conversation because of me, you could have continued it. Yes things are getting out of hand and whatever drug transaction went wrong this needs to be handled in a different way; perhaps a peaceful mediation," I said as my father looked at me like I had grown two heads.

"What are you talking about Rose?"
"Just what I said, I'm not a kid, and I'm not fragile so you don't have to lie to me," I said taking a bite of my burger.

"Baby this isn't some game that can be resolved that easily, this shit is serious and somebody can and will get hurt. What happened at your house won't even scratch the surface of what else they'll do to each other. A funeral is next," he said.

"A funeral! Can't you talk to Uncle Bo and I'll talk to Julian, so they come together and resolve to resolve this," I said.

"Listen to me Gabriela and listen well, because this about to be the truest realist shit I've ever said to you but it needs to be said. You pregnant with that nigga's baby, and I have a feeling you'll only be here temporarily even though I would love for you to stay forever. But, you need to know exactly what you up against so you won't do nothing stupid like the shit that just came out of your mouth. Legend had no idea Silas was your uncle because I'm positive had he known when he first met you, he would have put a bullet in your head," he said.

"Why?" I asked as my eyes grew big once I said that he was serious.

"I know because that's how the game go in this line of work. I know because I would have done the same thing," he said to me as my mouth dropped open. Before I could speak, he held his hand up signaling me to be quiet as he kept talking.

"You said stop shielding you from reality, so that's the real reality of it all. If Legend didn't love you, you would have died Friday. But, how he acted at your house lets me know you're at least safe with him because he damn sure won't let anything happen to you. But, if you gone choose to stick by him, you need to most definitely stay out of this shit between him and Bo. Trust me you start bringing him having a sit down, he gone start thinking crazy and then I'll have to kill his ass," he said.

"Daddy! Have you really killed someone before?"

"It's a lot about me you don't know princess but let's just say your birth and your mother's death changed me for the better. I gave up that lifestyle and took all the illegal money I had made and did what your mother had been asking me for years to do, invested it. I had to be a better man for you," he said as his eyes got sad just at the mention of my mother's name.

"So you was into drugs as well? Is that why you didn't like Chance or Julian?" I asked him.
"Enough question and answer for one day, feed my grand baby," he said but his lack of response told me all I needed to know. Things in my life kept getting my complex by the minute, but after talking to the most important people in my life, I at least had a better understanding of it.

****

"Thank you for that information," I said clicking my phone to hang up the Air Pods as a fax came through on my father's fax machine.

Grabbing the papers, I read over it with a smile on my face as I rolled in his office chair back to his desk.

"Here eat this, you've been in this office all morning," my step mother said walking into the office carrying a tray of food and orange juice as my stomach instantly starting growling reminding me I had not eaten at all today.

"Sorry ma, I got sidetracked working on something," I said with a smile as I graciously accepted the food.

"When you get in these moods, you go hours without eating, you gone wind your hard headed ass up back in the hospital. You eating for two Gabs, you have to remember that," she said as I bite into what tasted like heaven.

"I know ma and I'm sorry it won't happen again," I said with my hand over my mouth chewing my food.

"I know that look, I'll leave you alone, but don't make me beat your ass about my grand baby," she said threatening me before kissing me on the forehead and leaving back out the office.

Taking another bite of my food, I put the sandwich down as I went back to typing on the computer as I pressed print before stopping to take another bite. My phone began ringing as I clicked answer on my phone without looking down to see who was calling.

"Hello?" I said pressing print on the document I was working on.

"I hope you enjoyed your vacation because it's over. You got about ten minutes to have all your shit packed up before I pull up," Julian said.

Hearing his voice surprising made me smile. I would be lying if I said I hadn't been waiting on him to call me since yesterday when my two days was up.

"Oh so I haven't heard from you all this time and you didn't show up when you said you was because this was a vacation for me?" I said with a fake attitude knowing I wasn't really mad.

I had barely been sleeping because I had gotten so used to sleeping with him every night that now sleep wasn't the same for me.

"I've been busy, I ran into some issues while I was away, and had to get some shit straight when I got back home. Listen bruh I don't have time to hear your damn mouth today, you got eight minutes now to be ready. I'm telling you Gabriela don't make me come inside that damn house and show my ass," he said.

"How you even know where my parents stay?"

"I know everything it's nothing you can do without me knowing remember that," he said.
"You think you know everything," I said just to mess with him.

"Try me and see that bruh like I said I've had a long day and I'm not in the mood, you got five minutes now, less talking and more packing. I don't hear shit being moved in the background," he said.

"That's because I never unpacked like you said, so I'll be ready when you get here zaddy," I said cutting the attitude act because I was far from mad and really had missed him.

Being away from him after we have so recently connected had me feeling things I tried not to admit. Even when I was mad at him thinking he had done something to my uncle, I still wanted him near me. I'm sure my answer shocked him because I wasn't arguing back with him which fucked his head up because the line got quiet. So quiet, I thought he had hung up.

"Hello? Julian?" I said suddenly second guessing myself. I had to run the conversation back in my head to make sure I didn't say the wrong thing to him.

"Zaddy huh?" He said with laughter in his voice.

"Yes," I said in a low voice as I got up gathering all of my things out of the office before I made my way out the door and up the stairs to my room.

"Oh yeah? You saying that shit like you ready to take this dick all night, a nigga backed up too," he said instantly causing me to soak my panties just thinking about it.

"That's exactly what I'm saying," I said then giggled to myself because that's definitely something I've never been bold enough to in the past.

It's only been one day but it seemed like when I let go of all the things that was holding me back from truly experiencing and enjoying life, everything seemed much simpler. I didn't have to over think my responses to people and or dwell so hard on a situation. It felt quite liberating, and was giving me that same care free feeling I had in Jamaica. The feeling when I abandoned all morals and had an amazing week with a stranger who turned out to be exactly what my life was missing. Telling Julian I would be ready when he got here, I ended the call as I hurried gathered all of my bags together making two trips downstairs setting everything by the door, well everything I planned on bringing with me. My step mom had went baby shopping crazy and purchased so much stuff already that I couldn't possibly bring all of that with me. Plus I bought some things myself off line which came in early today.

"Let me guess, that fuck nigga about to pick you up?" My father said as I made my last trip downstairs and noticed him putting his keys on the table indicating he had just gotten home.

"Yeah it's better to go with him then put up a fight because he wouldn't let me stay if I wanted to," I truthfully said even though I really wanted to go.

"The hell he wouldn't! If you don't want to go you damn sure don't have to. I wish the fuck he would walk up in this bitch and try and move you, he gotta move and first! And that damn sure ain't gone be easy no matter how old I am!" My father barked his voice so loud it bounced off all the walls in the house.

"Daddy it's ok really I want to go, I miss him. I don't want to be in the middle of this stuff with him and uncle Bo, it's not fair to me nor my baby. Don't be mad at me," I said.

"Come here baby girl," he said pulling me into his arms in a big hug. "Listen I won't lie to you and said shit about to calm down with those two, but Bo already know how I give it up when it comes to you and he loves you just as much as I do. So, even though those two not gone stop trying to kill each other, neither one will let you be in in harm's way. But I'm telling you now if you walk out that door and go down that road, even though your uncle still loves you, your relationship will never be the same. I'm not telling you this to say choose him, I'm telling you this because you said stop lying to you, so I'm keeping it real with you. I'll never stop loving you and you will always be my daughter and welcome anywhere I'm welcome. But this war too far gone and your uncle although he'll never hurt you I know he gone take this like a slap in the face and it's just honesty how this game goes. If you had chosen your Uncle Bo over Legend, he would have definitely been there for his child but he would have never fucked with you again," my dad said dropping a heavy weight on me that I definitely wasn't prepared for.

Maybe being truthful with me wasn't the right thing move because this one definitely was more than I could bare. My uncle was like my best friend, and bonus daddy, he's always been there for me no matter what, and we had an amazing relationship.

"Can you at least talk to him for me daddy that's not fair," I whined.

"It's the life you chose you Princess this how the game go when you get caught up in a love with a dope boy and not a square ass suit and tie nigga," he said. "Wait right here before you leave, I bought something for you, I didn't know you was leaving this early because I had planned on giving it to you tomorrow," he said walking off.

Even though he had made it perfectly clear his position and where he stood, this still felt like I was saying goodbye to my family, my old life, and my peace. Rubbing my stomach, I willed the tears not to fall as I stood waiting for my father to come back down. A few seconds later he walked back up carrying a case as he took his head holding my chin up.

"You Big Los daughter, flesh of my flesh, my blood runs through your veins, you hold them fucking tears in and don't you dare let them fall you hear me! That soft shit stops today, you wanted people to be honest with you, you wanted this life, the weak get chewed up and spit back out. I've shielded you from this world your whole life and I see I can't protect you forever; what I should have done was bred a warrior but in your own way you are a warrior. You stronger than you give yourself credit for and sometimes being somebody no one can fuck with isn't about fighting or shooter, it's about wits and out smarter a person. The goal is always to be the last man standing, remember that, if it's between you and them bet on yourself every time princess," he said handing me the case and I opened it revealing a gun.

"Daddy I don't want this! Is this loaded?" I asked him all dramatically.

"Hell yeah it's loaded and you gone take the shit, because in this world snakes come in all forms and it doesn't even have to be your fight for you to be pulled into it. People will try and get at Legend through you so therefore you have to be on guard at all times. Remember I used to take you to the gun range for fun when you were little?" He said.

I remember those days all too well, I always just assumed it was friendly father daughter bonding. I never would have imagined I was preparing for something. As my phone began to ring, I already knew it was Julian calling me as I let it ring out to voicemail as I answered my father.

"Yes, you always said aim high miss low."

"Keep your eyes open on your target at all times and shoot to kill because letting somebody live can and will come back to bite you. Also don't think because you are in a certain place that you're safe, not even inside your own home. You safe here because Bo ass know I'll take it there that's why I don't give a fuck if Legend know where I lay my head or not. Los don't run from nigga, I'm still about all that dumb shit," he said.

I have never heard him talk like this in my life, like wow people really only showed me a side of them that they wanted me to see. This shit was crazy. My phone started to ring again and again I let it ring out to voicemail as my father continued talking. At this point my step mom had come downstairs.

"Stop all of that Carlos you scaring my baby," she said.

"She not a baby Lilian, she grown as hell, making grown woman decisions in a grown man business, the same shit you had to do when I met you and you were a school teacher. You know what come with this shit. I sat my ass down some for my daughter but you know it took me a long ass time to fully get out. You've been riding with me plenty of times when a nigga tried to off my ass, hell they even tried to shoot the church one time when we were at war with them fools from out west. Over reason shit even calmed down was when Bo moved and our crews on here in the city. That took the heat off me and shifted their focus a bit," he said.

"I don't care about none of that, I love Gabriela like she slide out of me and I'll die protecting my baby, that's on me! You better make sure not a hair on her fucking head is harmed," she yelled at him.

"Woman you act like my damn fight you know how that shit go so calm that gangsta down," he said back to her giving her a look that said don't test me.

She looked like she wanted to say more but didn't and I hated the fact that they were fighting and it was because of me. "BOOM! BOOM! BOOM! GABRIELA BRING YOUR ASS ON BRUH I TOLD YOU I DONT MIND SHOWING MY ASS!" I heard Julian say as I put my gun into my big brown checkered Louis Vuitton bag next to the files I stuffed in there.

"Oh this nigga done lost his muthafuckin mind beating on my shit like that," my father said going to the door and throwing it open to a very pissed off Julian.

He looked past my father from me to my mother to all my bags lined up by the door.

"I was talking to my parents, you didn't even have to do all of that, I said coming," I snapped annoyed at him not making the situation better.

"Say nigga, the only reason me and you ain't had no damn problem yet is because I want my grandchild to have a father and I know it would break my daughter's heart if I put you down, but don't keep testing me lil nigga," my father said to Julian who needed even blink nor seem intimated in the least bit.

The only thing he did was smirk as he got that same crazy look in his eyes that he had before he pulled the trigger that night in my house.

"Naw old head, you got shit backwards, the only reason you ain't eating a bullet to the dome that day was because of my girl, I don't give a fuck about my son not having no grand daddy."

"Son?" I'm having a boy?" I said in shock and disbelief that he had found out before me and not with me. When Julian realized what he has accidentally let slip out, he genuinely looked sad and apologetic, something that was rare for him.

"It's a boy? Hell yeah," my pops said like the last few minutes didn't just happen at all as he actually dapped Julian up.

"Let me go start adding boy clothes to my cart," my step mom said.

"Woman you better not bring shit else into this house yet, you've always ordered enough," my father said stepping aside as Julian came and grabbed all of the bags up.

I'm not sure how he did it, but he literally had all of them in his hands as he walked off to the car. Hugging my parents, I told them I would be back by in a few days as my father made me promise to remember what he said.

"I promise," I said as he walked me outside. Getting into the car, a feeling of calmness and safety washed over me. I felt safe anywhere Julian was and prayed to God I was never put in a situation where I would have to keep that promise I made to my parents.

******

After riding in silence a half hour, I finally spoke up and said, "You didn't have to do all that back there, I told you I was all pocked up and ready to go. I was talking to my father," I said.

I almost slipped up and told him what the conversation was about, but my daddy's words rang out loudly in my ness about not discussing Bo with Julian.

"I told ya ass you had five minutes; you could have called him from the car. I'm tired and I've had a long day," he said. Again, I started to be my usual combative self, but Destiny screaming in my head to be his peace, made me reroute myself.

"What happened today?" I asked leaning over playing in my dreads something he loved when I did.

"Just a whole lot of a whole lot. I had to make sure everything at the house was straight and set up for everybody," he said.

"You didn't have to get new furniture or anything fancy, and I don't mind helping you clean up baby," I said.

"I switched houses; I still have my old house though."

"I thought you said your house was like three bedrooms?" I said.

"Yeah we needed something bigger so we wouldn't be all up on each other. Plus I wanted to be off the grid a little bit more," He said not offering any further explanation to this new house.

"We? I thought this was a temporary arrangement?" I asked him because I had no idea he was thinking of us living together long term.

"Just roll with the flow bruh, you always gotta question shit," he said.

"I was just asking for clarity on our status and where we stand. We never really sat down and discussed any of it. That's typically how things work," I shot back.

I know I was supposed to be arguing less with Julian but if trusting him and being his peace meant I couldn't still have opinions on things, this wasn't gone completely work for me. I didn't have a problem changing because I realized what I was doing wasn't working for me, but I refuse to not be able to think for myself at least.

"Damn let a nigga get to that damn part and just learn to damn chill out sometimes. You so used to that fuck boy that you had that you don't know just to just sit back and relax and let a man be a man. How you act, I know you ain't used to what a nigga like me can do for you and before you open your mouth I don't just mean financially. I know you got your own bread and I respect that shit, but a real nigga reaches for his wallet before a woman can even bend down to grab her purse," he said.

Since he was slightly right about that sense for and bought everything for Chance, I accepted defeat and dropped the subject. For this to work I was going to have to relinquish control and one hundred percent let Julian lead and I follow which would definitely be a challenge but I was up for it.

"Besides moving, how was your day?" I asked him.

"Shit just long that's all, nigga tired as hell, I ain't had a good night's rest in a minute."

"Me either, I can't sleep without you besides me. I've gotten so spoiled and used to use cuddling me tightly against you sleeping that my body craves it, or rather maybe your child misses its daddy," I said.

"Naw you just daddy that's all ma it's ok to admit it."

"Oh I definitely did," I said reaching over putting my hands inside the sweat pants he was wearing. Never had I been so bold with him as I began to stroke him through his boxers as I heard him suck in a deep breath.

"Oh that's how you doing it? I want to keep this same energy when we step foot inside of that house. You know what's up with me, don't play with it if you ain't ready for these problems. I got some pressure backed up so I'm tryna murder the pussy all night long," he said making my body shutter.

"And just like I told you when we first met, I want all those problems," I said.

The entire time I was talking to him, I had begun to take my seatbelt off as I bodily took his dick out of his boxers at the same time as I leaned my entire body over the seat moving myself to a position where I could do what my mouth was watering to do. It's crazy to go from never having experienced oral sex to fucking somebody who you physically craved doing it to.

"Fuck," Julian moaned out the second I spit on his dick and took him into my mouth.

Apparently I had forgotten in a few short days how big he was because I attempted to put too much in my mouth too fast and damn near choked myself as I relaxed my mouth and jaw and tried it again this time taking him down my throat as far as I could go.

"Suck that dick just like that girl," Julian said as he pulled his pants down further moving the clothes that were somewhere restricting me out of the way.

I raised up, slapped his dick on either side of my face a few times, before paying special attention to the tip of this dick. I'm not sure about other guys, but me licking the tip of Julian's dick always drove him insane. At one point I started French kissing the tip making love to it with my mouth before I spit on his dick again and slurped him down my throat as I used both of my hands to massage his dick up and down while rotating my mouth around in a circle. The entire time I was doing this I was moaning louder than Julian as I felt his hands sliding in between my legs. Even though I was fully clothed with a onesie one, I still felt the effects of what his fingers were doing to me playing with my pearl. How this was even possible with clothes on just showed me exactly how skilled of a lover he really was.

"Oh shit stop it girl before you make me fucking nut," he said as I felt his legs tensing up.

That only made me go harder as increased the suction of my mouth going fast up and down as I came up for a brief second and spit on his dick massaging it up and down then took him back down my throat. Once I touched his balls massaging them gently, I felt like that was his breaking point as he forcefully snatched me by my hair trying to get me to get up, which I always did before this part. However, I shook him off ass I kept going because Destiny had told me once you suck a guy's nut into your mouth like a champ, you'll have him hooked.

"Fuck you nasty bitch you gone catch all this nut? Fuckkkk catch all of it then baby just like that girl," he said as I continued sucking feeling something warm shooting into my mouth.

Once I felt like I had milked him dry, I released his dick and sat up looking him dead in his eyes following the remainder of the instructions Destiny gave me as I opened my mouth wide letting him see all of his semen in it as I closed my mouth and swallowed all of it. He just looked at me stuck for a few seconds until a horn blowing alerted us of incoming traffic and he swerved to avoid a car.

"That better be some shit that gay nigga taught you cuz if you did that to that bitch ass nigga from the restaurant you and his ass is dead," he said.

I don't know how we went from what just happened to him threatening me, but since Destiny said this also might happen if I did it correctly, I simply smiled satisfied with myself.

"I can't wait to get to the fucking house," he said fixing his clothes but never taking his eyes off the wheel again. I can't wait either I thought to myself as I put my head back on the seat. That took a lot out of me and it wasn't even a lot so I needed to take a little nap to get myself prepared for what was to come soon as we got home. Home, I liked the sounds of that.

*****

"Wake that was up," I heard.

I don't know how long I'd been sleep, but it felt like I had gotten a few hours nap when I knew we couldn't have possibly been driving that much longer.

"I didn't realize I was that tired," I said stretching my arms as I looked out my window seeing nothing but trees all around me.

I was so engulfed in trying to recognize the neighborhood to guess my location, that I almost missed the huge mansion up ahead in the circular driveway.

"Oh my God this is the house!" I said.
"Yeah you like it baby?"

"I freaking love it! This house is insane it's like a mansion!" I said because this made even his huge estate in Jamaica look like a duplex compared to how big this house was. It had to have cost way over a few million easily.

"I'm glad you like it, now enough talking let's go," he said putting the car in park getting out as he opened the back door and grabbed my bags out as I grabbed my purse and got out as well.

As we headed towards the house, I pulled my phone out shooting my parents a group text letting them know we had made it safely and I would speak with them tomorrow. By the time I put my phone away, Julian already had the door open as I walked in to a beautiful sight. The foyer was even beautiful bare and all. Walking straight ahead, I was giving myself a quick tour as I followed behind Julian. The foyer and hallway opened up to an emasculate floor plan that was huge and beautifully crafted. I noticed it was barely furniture anywhere just little odds and ends here and there. Straight ahead were a pair of beautiful double winding stairways on either side of the room both leading upstairs. Continuing to take everything in, I began to picture where I would put things if I was allowed to help decorate.

"What color scheme did you go with for the living room?" I asked Julian following him up the stairs.

"I didn't. I grabbed a few things here and there but I figured if you was gone be living here, I would let you pick out the decorations. I know women like that sort of thing. All my cribs look the same, black with gold trimmings," he said.

Him actually including me in this and giving me the option to pick out color schemes and decor really made me love him even more as my heart swelled with joy. I loved to decorate so this was about to be so fun! Everything leading up to this point completely wiped away from my mind because nothing else mattered anymore.

*****

Once we got into the room, Julian got a call on his phone as he stepped out of the room to take it. I wanted to explore this house as I had done in Jamaica, but right now I was hungry and was hoping he at least had some food in the kitchen. Sitting my bag down on the bed, I made a mental note to tell Julian about the good news I had found out for him. I was sure this would not only get him to finally trust me and open up to me more, but it would also take a lot of his current stress away. Putting my phone on the charger, I made my way back down the stairs in search of the kitchen. It didn't take me long however to find it because of the aroma of food smell that hit my hungry ass as soon as my foot touched the last step. Walking into the kitchen, I saw an older yet gorgeous woman taking food out of the oven wrapped with foil paper.

"Hello," I said to her. I wasn't sure if she was the cook, or a maid or something.

"Hail gyal cum sidung an nyam yuh need food luk at yuh standing there all skin an bones ow cya mi grand pickney grow wen him starving.(Hello girl, come sit down and eat. You need food, look at you standing there all skin and bones. How can my grandchild grown when he is starving) she said.

I instantly knew she was from the island, so that meant she either had to be Julian's mother or his aunt or something. Looking down at the onesie I wore, I instantly became embarrassed because I looked a mess, and my hair was all over my head. I definitely didn't want to meet his relatives looking like this as a first impression.

"Come," she said again fixing me a huge plate literally piled to the top with all sorts of food.

My stomach instantly growled looking at it all as I eagerly walked in further and sat down on a stool at the island bar. As soon as she slid the plate in front of me, I picked up my fork digging in. The food was so delicious, and instantly reminded me of Jamaica. The authenticity of the dishes was something I could definitely get used to.

"This is very good, thank you for this. I didn't realize exactly how hungry I was," I said putting my fork down.

I still had a lot of food on my plate, and my fat ass planned on eating it, I was just taking a break because I had eaten so much so fast.

"Yuh welcome chile now nyam up,"(You welcome chile, now eat up) she said motioning for me to finish eating.

She definitely didn't have to tell me twice as I picked my fork back up while she fixed another plate which I'm assuming was for Julian placing it beside me as she took her apron off and walked out of the kitchen. By the time I had finished, she still had not come back as I got up to rinse my plate out and put it in the dish washer. Turning around I saw Julian walking into the kitchen.

"Baby that was so good. Oh my God I'm so sleepy and full, that food that I just had was amazing. Is that your mom? Oh my God I hope she stays for a long time; her food is to die for," I said rambling on and on as he walked up on me looking angry.

"What's wrong with you? What happened?" I asked him suddenly concerned.

"Bitch you come into my house and fucking try and play me! I should have known something was up how you was acting all different and shit in the car, then you sucked a nigga up," he said angrily as he grabbed me by my shirt hemming me up on the stainless steel refrigerator.

"Baby what are you talking about?" I said.

"Cut the act bruh what the fuck is this?" He said tossing the gun and files onto the bar. I looked down at them and looked back up into the barrel of a gun. **Shit.**

LEGEND

"Yeah get me everything you got on a nigga named Los that be with Silas," I said to Hal, a computer geek that I just put on my team today.

Tan was cool but she was more so the brains of my shit, she wasn't the find a nigga who disappeared, hack into the Feds computer system type. She had her own lane, and she did her shit well, I just needed somebody else more equipped to get done what I needed. Niggas kept managing to slip in and try and fuck my shit up, and if I wasn't the nigga that I was, I would be dead by now. Hal came highly recommended to me from my homeboy Danger out in Texas who had Dallas on lock. That nigga crazy as fuck and thorough bred, so if he said Hal good people than ima rock with his ass. So far he's proven in a few shorts hours to really be a big asset to my team.

"You'll have it in your email in ten minutes. I also already tracked the phone number you gave me, but it came back a burner number so the GPS signal on those not always accurate because they bounce off all type of towers and shit," Hal said.

When Gabriela had went to sleep on the drive over, I snuck into her phone and got Silas number out of it.

"Bet. You got them files I asked you about yet?"

"I'm working on it, the FBI got the shit locked up tighter than a virgin, with all types of encrypted passwords blocking my access, but ima get in soon," he said.

I had him looking into reports on Case's shit trying to see who tipped them off to even hit the truck he was in to begin with. Either somebody was dirty, or somebody was a damn informant, either way I was gone find out and send the information to Malechi's ass so he could get on that.

"Hit me back when you got something for me then," I said hanging up the phone as the motion detectors I had around the house alerted me that somebody was walking around.

Pulling up the cameras, I saw Gabriela's nosey ass walking down the stairs rubbing her belly as she headed into the kitchen. I couldn't wait for her to have my son, and then give me a daughter and about three more kids. I've always wanted a big family, that's why I had this house built in the first place. Once I decided it was time for me to get out of the game and I proposed to Myriah's hoe ass, I sat down and designed this house and then hired a crew to start bringing my vision to life. I knew it would take some years to be built because of all the shit I wanted done to it.

With the type of life that I lived, I needed something that was secluded, secure, spacious and fully equipped to the point it was no need to leave the house in case we had to lay low for a while. There were a total of four wings and two living quarters. Each quarter has its own living room, dining room, and four bedrooms and four bathrooms. Not only was the home sound proof, and bullet proof, but each wing has its own entrance as well.

There was also a gun range, movie theater, bowling alley, basketball court, game room, and a lot of more shit. I had intended to give it to Myriah as a wedding gift, and we would have moved in once it was done. Good thing I never even told her ass about it, though and when we broke up, instead of having them stop construction on the house, I allowed them to continue working on it. It took a few years for them to build it, but when they were done, instead of moving in it, I simply kept the maintenance up on it and made sure everything was up to date and in working order.

I had never even stepped foot in the house until earlier today, but shit it damn sure had come in handy after everything that went down yesterday in Jamaica. My momma no matter how big of a G she is, was still shaken up a bit after the shootout we were in. Shit I'm just lucky after all that shit that happened, we even managed to make it into Atlanta at all. I just knew after the stunt Silas pulled that he would have the airport sewed up with his men, or at the very least alert immigration or some hoe shit like that of my mother being in the country illegally.

So, when I stepped off of the jet at Hartsfield airport dressed in my disguise, I already had it in my mind that we were about to have to go with plan B in order to get my mother safely in the city. However, once I slipped through the airport and pretended to be working, everything else seemed to flow rather smoothly. The casket cleared customs, and was immediately taken by the funeral service I had hired to pick up the body. Instead of driving my mother back to the funeral home, they met me at an abandoned house. I paid them, and they carried a body back with them inside of the casket. The body switch was last minute thought of just in case somebody was to look into it, they would see that a body did arrive, and the family requested a cremation.

DING!DING

An incoming email on my iPad snapped me out of my day dream as I clicked on the link Hal had sent me as I got up to head to my room to shit before I went downstairs to buss down this plate of food I knew my mom made for me. My iPad went dead as I was in the bathroom as I was reading everything Hal sent me about Los ass. So, when I came out, I noticed Gabriela had plugged her phone up to charge, so I took hers off charger for a bit and put my iPad on charger so I could get enough juice to finish reading the email. I didn't feel like finding my own damn charger just yet. Sitting on the edge of my bed with one leg hanging off the side, and one thrown across the bed, I sat back against my pillows trying to get comfortable as my iPad powered back on. That's when I felt something hard under my back and realized I was laying on her purse.

"This shit heavy as fuck, what the fuck she got in this bitch," I said as I picked her purse up and tossed it on the night stand on side of the bed.

However, when I put it up there, the shit fell over, and all the bullshit she had in it fell out as well. I didn't think anything of it as I bent down to pick all the shit up until something caught my eye. You would think it would have been the gun that was laying there that had pissed me off, however, it was the words on the stack of papers lying beside the gun that caught my attention.
"This snake ass bitch," I roared picking the gun and glancing over the papers before marching out of the room heading downstairs into the kitchen.

The minute I seen Gabriela; I hemmed her little ass up as I tossed the shit on the counter at the same time as I pulled my own gun out on her. With so much shit going on in these streets, it was to the point where anything done damn sure was no longer a coincidence. Shit had definitely gotten real, and I needed to know who she was riding with. I know it was fucked up to make her choose between me and her peoples, but that's exactly what the fuck I was doing. This shit ain't a game, niggas tried to dead ass take me and my momma out yesterday, so she wasn't about to be sitting up in my shit on no snake shit. Find her ass chopped up into little pieces on her people door step, fuck she thought this was.

"Wait Julian I can explain, it's not whatever it looks like," she said.

"It's exactly what the fuck it looks like ma, since when you started carrying a tool around with? And that bitch loaded! So that shit in the car just now was an act huh? Sucked a nigga soul out his dick and then what? You was gone come home, fuck me to sleep, then off me? Then let your people's go get at my brother? You got paperwork stating exactly what prison and pod he in and shit? I see what type of game y'all bitch asses on! Yesterday's attempted hit on my life ain't work, so they used my bitch and my baby against me because y'all the only people who could have gotten close to me and you really in on this shit!" I yelled.

The more my brain came up with crazy scenarios, the angrier I became as my hands slipped from her collar to her neck. Usually when I'm choking her, it's not to hurt her, I just be hitting her ass with some death strokes and choking her at the same time. However, this time when I grabbed her neck, I wanted the bitch to stop breathing. I had risked it all for her and my baby and this how she tried to play me. Everything I did, I did for her. I could have had my niggas run up in her parent house guns blazing bussing at everything breathing, laying everybody down in sight not caring if that fuck niggas Silas was in that bitch or not. But, I didn't because I knew shawty and her parents was there and I ain't have no smoke with them. And because I love shawty I think, but I keep getting played each time I think I loves these hoes. Fuck love! Love really will get you killed! As I watched her hitting my arms struggling to breathe and explain herself, I tried to will myself to let her go in order to listen to explanation, but I don't know what took over my body. My brain heard me, but it refused to cooperate with what the fuck I was telling it to do.
BAM! BAM! My mother hit my ass about six damn times in the back of my head with something before I released Gabriela and turned around.

"What you hit me for ma?"

"Yuh tun dat gyal lose what's wrong wid yuh boy! mi didn't raise yuh tuh put yuh hands pan girls! yuh fada needs fi get out an get fi him boys y'all ave lose yuh damn minds! an shi carrying mi grand pickney."(You turn that girl lose what's wrong with you boy! I didn't raise you to put your hands on girls! Your father needs to get out and get his boys y'all have lost your damn minds! And she is carrying my grandchild) she said.

"Shi sitting up here pan sum snake shit ma! shi working wid di enemy dat try tuh tek wi out an yuh gaan side wid har,"(She sitting up here on some snake shit ma! She working with the enemy that tried to take us out and you gone side with her)

"Yuh aks har?"(Did you ask her)

"No I didn't ask her ass but I got the proof I need," I said turning back around to look at Gabriela who was sucking in big gulps of air.

"Did you really just assault me because you not fucking man enough to open your mouth and ask before you fucking react to some shit when I was trying to help alleviate some of your stress," Gabriela yelled looking me dead in my eyes.

Her little ass might talk reckless, but she never talked this crazy to me. I knew I wasn't trippin', so instead of responding to what she said, I picked the papers up and tossed them her way.

"Explain, cuz when one plus one don't equal two fucking right a nigga gone jump from zero to hundred. Stopping to analyze and act fucking questions in the line of work I'm in will get your killed quick as fuck. Ain't nobody talking shit out thinking rationally," I said as her face softened like she really understood me or some shit even though I had never had that conversation with her about what it is I actually did.

"I know and your right I'm sorry," she said further surprising me. Before I could say speak on how her ass was acting different, she kept talking.

"I know what it is you do for a living, and I know people in my life you included treat me different trying to shield me from the evils of life. I don't want people to walk on egg shells around me and I want you to be able to trust me with the truth rather than dancing around a lie. I don't know what it is between you and my uncle, but I know it's illegal. However when I walked out of my parent's house today, I made the decision to be with you. I actually chose my family way before my father made me understand that this was an unspoken choice choosing you. To me even though it hurt me to do so, I realized I would chose you every time. I never knew Case was in jail until Stacy told me. Destiny told me I needed to be your peace and maybe you wouldn't hide shit from me. So, when I found out that Case was in jail, I did what I did best, I looked into his case for you," she said making me feel like shit for not even asking her before I jumped to conclusions when she was really out here showing a nigga she was ready to ride for me. I had never really had that before.

Sure Myriah acted like she was loyal, but this shit Gabriela just did was pure love and loyalty. I had been struggling with ways to approach her about Case, and here it was she took it upon herself to do it for me just to help. This shit confirmed the internal battle I had been having with myself about her. I loved this fucking girl.

"I ain't never apologized to no fucking body in my life, I don't even know how to do that shit bruh, but with everything in me I apologize for jumping to conclusions without asking you. Shit is so crazy right now and it's getting worse by the minute. I went to get my mom from Jamaica because she wasn't safe and we damn near didn't make it back to the plane with our life," I said not bothering to go more in-depth with my explanation.

Regardless of her now knowing what I did, I still didn't want knowing every aspect of this life.

"Oh my God why didn't you tell me! Are you ok?" She asked me walking up to me checking me all over from head to toe as I stood there in amusement.

Once she was satisfied with her inspection, she stepped back a bit and just looked at me. That raw emotion that I saw in her eyes made me know right then and there that this girl was my rib, somebody I would lay my life down for. Without saying another word, I leaned down and kissed her passionately. I almost forgot my mother was in the kitchen as well as I picked Gabriela up by her thighs sitting her in the counter.

"Si communication Julian,"(See communication Julian) my mother said. "An yuh gyal yuh betta nuh let him chat tuh yuh crazy or put fi him hands pan yuh yuh guh upside fi him head an sex isn't a reward fi a apology yuh hold out fi a gift,"(And you girl, you better not let him talk to you crazy or put his hands on you. You go upside his head and sex isn't a reward for an apology. You hold out for a gift) she said.

"Don't listen to her ass," I said kissing down Gabriela's neck as my mother took her by the arm pulling her off with her.

"Cum pan help mi wid sup'm,"(Come on help me with something)

"How you gone cock block your own child ma? That's wild yo," I said straightening my hard dick inside my shorts as I grabbed all the papers off the floor taking them with me to the counter as I grabbed a fork and sat down to eat while reading over them.

About an hour and thirty minutes later, I found myself in the room still going over the files trying to make sense of them as Gabriela finally came walking back into the room.

"Your mother is a so great, I love her," she said. She was now wearing some pajamas shorts and a shirt.

"When did you change?"

"When you were downstairs still eating, I came in to grab a quick shower before I went back over to Ma side. I love her quarters," she said walking over to the bed as I swung my legs over the side opening them up and pulling her between them.

"Ma huh?"

"Yeah she said I could call her that. You don't mind do you?" She asked me.

I had no doubt that her and my mother would get along because Gabriela was genuinely a cool person and my mother could sense when somebody spirit wasn't right. She couldn't stand Myriads hoe ass for shit and seeing how everything played out, she had every right not to like her. That's why I only brought Myriah to Jamaica once to see her. The fact she instantly took to Gabriela was good because when I broke the news to her on the plane that she was going to be a grandmother, I didn't know how her ass would react once she saw her.

"Yeah but don't listen to nothing she says," I said laughing.

My mom may have appeared to be sweet but she didn't take no shit and was crazy. I didn't want her turning my girl that way.

"Well she's right, you jumped to conclusions without even talking to me, so I'll take a black Birkin bag tomorrow and then we can finish what we started tonight," she said.

"Girl quit playing and come here," I said grabbing her around her waist pulling her closer into my legs as I raided her shirt up and kissed all over her stomach. "Hey daddy's baby, you hear yo momma tryna hoe me out here and shit?"

"Julian! That's not baby language," she said laughing.

"Woman hush my damn son understands me. Don't you son?" I said licking and kissing all over her stomach.

"I don't know why he always choosing the times when you

touch my stomach to want to kick," she said as I saw little feet pushing on her stomach.

There was really something inside of there, like I really had a new found respect for women at this point! This shit was beyond amazing to watch. Rubbing all over her stomach while she stood in between my legs, I moved my hands up higher to massage her breast trying to get mannish with her as she pushed my head away.

"Nope, get me my purse first," she said as my son chose that time to kick her again.

"Oh Trey that hurts," she said.

"Who the hell is Trey?" I asked immediately getting angry as I pinched her nipple.

"Trey is the nickname I gave him, and ouch," she said.

"Naw what nigga named Trey you thinking about? Is it that square ass nigga from the restaurant?" I said as she rolled her eyes at me.

"Roll them bitches again," I said.

"Julian Santiago the third or Trey, Jesus why are you like this," she said making me feel stupid.
"So, every day I gotta fight to prove my love," I shot back because I didn't have any real comeback. We both started laughing as Trey kicked her ass again.

"That's right daddy baby kick the shit out of your mean ole momma," I said as I went back to kissing on her stomach. I was about to slide lower and French kiss that pussy until she farted.

"Excuse me," her ass had the nerve to say before she burst out laughing as I pushed her ass away from me.

"Man you need to check your damn panties I know you shit on yourself," I said as she tried to hug on me while still laughing.

"Don't do that I just have gas it's the baby," she said.

"Don't blame what just came out of your ass on my lil nigga," I said.

"You still love me though," she said sticking her tongue out at me.

"I do, but I would love for your ass to go check yo drawers with your shitty ass," I said pushing her head playfully away from me.

I can't deny I haven't felt this relaxed and at peace in a while. This shit with Gabriela was pure and it came natural, and I was loving every minute of it. The more time I spent with her, the more I was ready to end this shit so I could focus on my family. As Gabriela walked into the bathroom, I checked my cameras making sure everything was straights as I pressed a button turning the kitchen and living room lights off and setting the entire house on night vision mode. An intruder couldn't see, but my cameras could and still would catch them. When Gabriela came back out the bathroom, I said,

"So you really not gone give me none of my pussy?"

"You just called me shitty," she said laughing.
"I'll hit you in the shower, it's cool," I said laughing as she tossed a pillow at me as she got on the bed moving the papers out of the way.

"Baby help me understand everything I'm looking at," I said as my mind got back to the task at hand.

"Well baby when I pulled everything up at my first intentions were only to look into the records because I knew you would have hired a good attorney for Case and two eyes are better than one. But, after I found out he didn't have an attorney yet," she was saying before I interrupted her.

"What makes you think he don't have an attorney? I dropped

fifty bands so for on one."

"You did? When?" She asked with her eyes brows raised.

"The first day he went in there," I said.

"You sure?" She said.

"I'm positive, what the fuck," I said not directing my anger at her but not liking the way the conversation going.

"I mean with the amount of money you paid him or her, I would have thought they would have at least did their due diligence in regards to the case," she said.

"Like get him a bond and shit because he tried, they were denied three times," I said.

"Well of course they were denied baby, look at the charges. However, any lawyer would have filed a motion to suppress evidence, and requested a bail hearing. From the looks of it Case has never had any prior convictions and the law doesn't allow anyone who isn't a flight risk nor a threat to society a denial of bond. That's a direct violation of his constitutional rights and any lawyer would have known this. Even someone charged with murder can get a bond, a lawyer would know this if they did their due diligence. It's a judge's job to deny bond in order to make that lawyer do his job," she said.

The way she spoke about law, her face lit up and she really came alive. This what my baby lived for, this that same reaction she had on them damn detectives.

"Baby you need to talk to him and make him do his job or file a complaint with the National Bad Association."

"Naw he canceled, you taking care of that," I said as the wheels in my head already began to turn with how I was about to cancel Malechi's ass for real.

"Julian it's not that simply, it's forms you have for fill out and

Case signs it, and," she said going on and on.

"Gabriela, listen to me you, Trey, ma, pops, Case and Cream are the only family I have out here in the free world. Family ride for family, and Case is your family now. We do everything we can to protect family. You know this law shit in your sleep, don't over think it, are you gone suit your and go get your hot headed baby brother?" I asked her looking deep into her eyes.

It's one thing to talk that talk, I needed to know if she was gone ride for a nigga.

"I need a brand new law office to go alone with my black Birkin bag," she said as I kissed her. Shit just got real.

****

"I heard about what's been going on, I can't wait to get the fuck up out of here up because shit is all fucked up right now. My hoes wilding', my girl talking about leaving me, and this food gone kill a nigga faster than a nigga will," Case said.

It had been a few days since I've talked to him because that bitch ass CO I had on payroll had been sick with the flu at home with his phone.

"Damn lil nigga that's tough," I said laughing.

"So you just gone laugh in my face like that? Gone mail me a steak these noodles taking me out," he said as we both burst out laughing cuz his ass hated noodles.

Shit I wouldn't wish a bid on nobody, cuz prison was ruthless but Case dead ass needed this reality check. I definitely was doing everything in my power to get him out, but I bet you he listen to my ass next time.

"You heard from your crew in there with you?" I asked.

"Just Justice since he got moved over here. He told me them other bitch ass niggas was over there crying and shit," he said.

"Man fuck all of that shit, none of that matters right now cuz I got some good news for you," I said.

"What you finally got me a bond and I'm coming home?"

"Soon, I got a surprise coming your way, be on the lookout for her. She coming to give you something," I said.

"You sending me a hoe to give me some ass? Shit ok then bro cuz I was tired of fucking these busted ass old ass guards. These hoes in this bitch smelling worse than niggas, but I'll close my eyes and take any pussy at this point," this ignorant nigga said.

"Nigga hell no nigga you stuck with them fishy pussy bitches," I said laughing.

"How ma doing?"

"Getting on my damn nerves beating my ass everyday about my baby. That's her problem she see you as a baby and not a man. A man who started a war I gotta try and finish and got my seed involved in this shit."

"Seed? What bitch you got pregnant?" He asked me.

I had been so busy I hadn't told him about running back into Gabriela or her being pregnant.

"Gabriela," I said.

"Gabriela? Gabriela. Ohh the bitch from Jamaica that ghosted yo ass! Yo you said fuck that hoe, so how she wind up pregnant? You hitting bitches raw now big bro? Not after you be chewing me out about the shit," he said.

"Say ima let it slide but let that be the last time you call my shorty a bitch," I said.

"Really nigga? As much as you call my girl a bald headed bitch?" He said.

"Oh that's different," I said laughing.

"Nigga fuck you, ima stop when you stop," he said as I heard loud commotion in the back.
"What's going on?" I said when I didn't hear anything, I called his name a few times before I heard the bitch ass guard I had on payroll come on the phone saying they had to go before hanging up. I wasn't tripping because at least I talked to him so I knew he was at least ok.

****

"Yo this shit nice as fuck," Cream said as we walked down to my man cave to politic before we headed to the warehouse to meet up with our crew.

I wanted to fill him in on everything right and get a clear understanding with him before we met up with them niggas.

"Yeah the shit better be nice, this really the definition of dropping a bag on something. This shit dead ass almost bankrupt my ass when I had it built, but I was thinking of the bigger picture at hand. I knew I could easily make the money back," I said.

"Hell yeah this definitely was a smart ass business move and a great investment, I gotta build me one next door," he said.

"Shit who you gone put in that muthafuckas? Stacy's ass," I said clowning him.

"You got jokes huh like you ain't been ring shopping for Gabriela," he shot back.

"Naw that's dead, I already gave one bitch a ring, I can finally admit I love her, and she giving me my first son, but this ain't that," I said.

"Love? Nigga you pussy whipped and shit," he said laughing.

"Shit least I got some pussy to be whipped off of," I said not even denying it because Gabriela had become my new addiction and

I couldn't get enough of her ass.

If she wasn't already pregnant, she definitely would be. The nympho in new craved her more than I've ever craved anything in my life. Funny thing is I just craved her, I didn't even have to penetrate her, I just needed her around me. Shit was gay as fuck but although I didn't understand it, it was easier not to fight the shit than keep denying these gay ass feelings and emotions.
"I'm knee deep in something every night nigga fuck you mean. Your confused ass was just acting like you ain't fuck with Gabriela, now that's bae," he said shaking his head.

"Just like you act like you don't give a fuck what Stacy got going on and who she fuck with," I said.

"Shit I don't, that ain't my pussy so who she giving it to ain't my business long as I got my place in line," his ass said but I could see through all that bullshit he was spitting I knew my brother really well; his ass would lose his shit if he saw her with somebody else.

He liked that damn girl he just didn't want to say it out loud because he didn't want it to be true. It wasn't because she was black because he loved black girls, shit that's all his as loved. Nigga was whiter than snow really out her convincing bitches he was just light skinned and shit. Naw he fucked ratchets but them not the type he wifed up. Shit Stacy lil slick mouth ass is the female, now I personally would have bodied shawty but he apparently like that shit he still fuck with her. Friends with benefits or not if a hoe got ways I don't like that I'm not doubling back for the pussy.

"Anyway nigga first things first, we gotta figure out this Silas problem because we took a major hit with them last time and we ain't got enough drugs to afford any more of our traps getting hit up," I said.

Because when our trap got hit, we lost close to twelve bricks.

That wouldn't be shit if we had bricks coming in, but we don't have shit to replace that with until I can secure a new connect. My name hold weight in these streets, so I'm not worried about getting one. Shit so hot right now for us, we too much of a liability business wise for anybody to fuck with. Case with this fed charge, this beef with Silas who got an army of niggas who gone keep gunning for us until I cut the head off the leader then all them bitches gone fall.

"Shit you know it's whatever with me I'll take on an army, but we damn aren't big enough as a unit to run down on that nigga," Cream said.

"I know that, we gotta hit that nigga where it'll make the biggest impact and let his ass know to stand the fuck down," I said.

"Man you know I ain't fucked up about fighting this nigga, but business wise we been eating good off his prices and product. Do you think we'll honestly get anything better?" He said.

I had been dreading him asking me this question because it had crossed my mind a few times already. But my pride wouldn't allow me to call truce on a war I didn't fucking start.

"When that nigga had them burn my momma house down, that deaded any communication we could have had. Them niggas tried to take my heart from me. I wasn't even fucking with his momma, I just let him know I knew where she laid her head at," I said.

"Didn't you say he said at Gabriela's house that he ain't get at yo mom's?"
"Shit yeah that's what that bitch made nigga said, but you was dodging bullets just like my ass, so clearly he lied. Who else we got beef with if it's not him?" I said.

"Shit I don't know, but have that new computer nigga you told me about to look deeper into that shit because we been knowing Silas, I don't fuck with him but he ain't even that type of nigga to throw stones and hide his hands like this. Nigga said he ain't send the hit, just verify that shit. Then, get Gabriela on it so she can bond Case out and that nigga just pay dude his money, you know you would be fucked up about that much bread as well," Cream said.

"Hell yeah I would dead a nigga on site but we ain't talking about just any nigga, we talking about my brother. I was always gone make Case make amends with Silas until he hit my trap and sent them people my momma way, now that's dead," I said.

"Well whatever long as the shit don't affect my bread," he said.

"Nigga you ain't nowhere near broke," I said.

"Shit and I'm tryna keep it that way, so is every other man on your team. You the boss, make an executive decision that's beneficial for the empire you said you not tryna see fall," he said.

I knew Cream was down to ride with me through whatever, but I also felt where he was coming from. Shit with shop closed up, my men wasn't feeding their families like they needed to. I had more money than I knew what to do with, so I was good with going to war with this nigga. I couldn't expect my team to be broke and wanna ride out.

"Cancel that meeting today. Tell Jaxson meet us at the warehouse so we can count up these bricks then open shop back up. We switching houses back to the old ones Mike was using," I said.

I haven't mentioned my nigga name out loud in a while and stopped using his traps when I murked him for fucking Myriah. I planned on taking Cream's advice and having Hal look into the Jamaica incident further. Even though I wanted to personally kill Silas and still probably would, we needed product so my team could eat. So, if he wasn't behind this shit, we was gone try work something out. But, that would mean somebody else was trying to get at us, but who?

****

"Baby you know I can't sleep without you here," Gabriela spoiled said.

For the first few nights of us living together, I was out till well into five the next morning. That's how shit went in these streets, but since she had my crazy ass momma in her ear telling her how to react, even though she knew the situation; her ass had started withholding the pussy. I don't know what my mom and pops had going on and how she handled shit with them, but ass a nigga who needed pussy like oxygen, I wasn't going for that shit. I knew I wasn't the best with communication because Myriah didn't require my ass to do none of that shit, and definitely didn't give a fuck when I came home. I had to make Gabriela's was understand I was gone fuck up if I didn't know I was fucking up. So I started making sure I was home every night at a decent time for a few nights, but that's ain't last long. I had shit to handle, and couldn't afford to do that and this family thing. Her ass can front all she wanted, she didn't want my ass at home, she just wanted this dick. I was slowly turning her ass out as well because she wanted the shit just as much as I did. She was always in the mood, no matter what time of day it was. She blamed it on the pregnancy and said her hormones were all over the place, but my cocky ass knew better.

"You just want this dick that's all," I said.

"Why you have to say it like that?" She said.

"Stop that shy shit what I tell you about that?" I said.

Her ass would be doing good with being my vocal, then would go back to being all shy. Don't be shy with me, tell me come fuck you to sleep. The day Gabriela tell me daddy come let me sit this pussy on your face, gone be the day I stop everything I'm doing and will grow wings and fly home if I have to.

"Baby," she whined.

"Open your mouth like a big girl or you ain't getting shit but the tip," I said.

"Ok you know I want it," she said. This shit sounded like Deja va when we was in the club on her birthday.

"Want what?"

"You to fuck me to sleep," she said causing my dick to instantly brick up.

"Daddy gone be home soon baby. You just better have that pussy wet and ready for me, cuz you know you gone have to back all this shit up you talking. I gotta go though, tell daddy baby calm his hyper ass down to," I said because I knew his ass was over there fucking her up.

My lil nigga stayed fighting and I was here for it. I wanted him to come out throwing them bitches punching other babies down and shit. I hung up just as Cream was shaking his head at me,

"Mind yo business ugly ass nigga and let's get this shit over me, I clearly gotta get home."

"Yeah you got a curfew and shit soft ass nigga," he said laughing.

I didn't even respond as I made sure I had everything I needed before getting out of the car that we had ducked off in some trees. Making sure the cost was clear, I pulled the black hoodie I was dressed in over my face a little as I ducked through the backyard, as Cream took the front. Hal had already found out the location of where this nigga was and had disarmed the alarm system while Tan had gotten us keys made so it definitely wouldn't look like a break in.

With my silencer on my gun, I came through the back door with my gun locked and loaded. It was just after midnight so I didn't expect these muthafuckas to be up, but you never know what to expect. I met Cream in the living room as we both looked at each other before tiptoeing up the steps. Hal had already told us which bedroom the nigga would be in and everything.

I'm telling you this nigga was worth every dime he asked me for and then some because his ass was proving to be a beast at what he did. If he ever turned on me I was for sure gonna have to get at his ass ASAP. A nigga like that could be a deadly enemy to have and I wouldn't hesitate to pop his little ass. Nigga was just like seventeen or some shit. Cream made it to the door before me as he waited for me to meet him at the door. Opening the door, just as I suspected, Malechi and his side bitch were inside of her bed sleeping peacefully without a care in the world. Under normal circumstances I would have put a pot of boiling water on and tossed it on their asses watching their skin melt off or some shit. But, I didn't have the time, energy, nor the patience to bullshit with this nigga.

Walking over to the bed, I took the butt of my gun and hit Malechi so hard I instantly broke his jaw as he yelled out so loudly in pain that it woke his bitch up. His old ass was married with kids and a daughter who just started college, yet he had a side bitch who was the daughter of a judge and young as his oldest daughter.

"What's going? Who are these people Malechi?" She said sitting up as the covers fell off her body revealing she was completely naked. I could tell everything on her was fake from the lips on down so I wasn't impressed. Looking at Cream and judging by the look on disgust on his face, neither was he. A real nigga ain't like all that fake ass shit, I'll take a stretch mark and cellulite over a plastic body any day of the week.

"Julian wha-aaat what is going on?" Malechi stuttered as I turned a lamp on. I had gloves on so I wasn't worried about my prints being on anything.

"Nigga cut the chit chat I don't have time for that bullshit. Snatch his ass up Cream, I got Malibu Barbie," I said moving to grab had as she started trying to plea bargain with me.

"Listen my father is a judge he'll pay you whatever you need if you don't hurt me. He'll make anything you need disappear," she said as I smirked and grabbed her by the hair as she started yelling and kicking.

I hit her twice in her face knocking her out.

"Please don't hurt her," Malechi said as I looked at him with an even grin grabbing her by her blonde hair literally dragged her ass out of the bed.

I didn't care that she hit the floor with a thump as I continued to casually drag her by her hair down every step until we made it to the living room. Cream pushed Malechi's ass down the stairs behind us as he crawled over to his bitch making sure her ass wasn't dead.

"What did I do? I promise I can fix it. I'm making great progress with the case," he said as I walked up to him standing him up just to knock his ass back down with a mean right hook.

After Gabriela confirmed what I had already suspected, it pissed me off for this night to sit in my face and play on my top like he was really out here trying to help my brother and shit. Bitch ass nigga wasn't doing shit but collecting a fucking check.

"Nigga you gone sit in my fucking face and lie to me!" I said.

"I'm not lying, this thing takes time like I told you. Just have patience and trust me," he said as Cream came back down with Malechi laptop handing it to him.

"What am I doing to do with this?" He said.

"Fill out the motion to withdraw from counsel paperwork and email me a copy, the judge a copy and anybody else you need to," I said.

"We can work this," he was saying until I hit his ass again.

"Nigga we can't work shit out now do what the fuck I said.

"Ok ok, you could have easily asked me to do that, you didn't have to do all of this," he said continuing to explain himself as he did what I asked.

I tuned his ass out at that point. I didn't need to hear no explanation from his ass because nothing he could say was gone let him walk away from this thing with his life. I just needed him to fill out those forms online requesting to withdraw as counsel. I didn't want to fire his ass because it would make it look too suspicious me firing him and then killing him. I never told Gabriela I was killing it him, I asked her what would be my option to not fire him even though he hasn't done shit for this case. I wanted him to appear mentally incompetent.

That's when she said have him do this motion to withdraw as counsel on the case bullshit and submit it online to the courts and email a copy to me. I then had Hal hack into his bank accounts as Tan transferred all of his money into an offshore accounts that if somebody did some digging they would eventually find. They could find the money, but they would never find Malechi's ass because I planned on pouring acid on his ass dissolving his body completely. That's why I had went through all of this, moving his money and shit. I didn't need any heat to come my way, so I would definitely make it appear like him and his young bimbo ran off with my money. She had to die as well, no face no case, she just was in the right place at the wrong time fucking around with the wrong married nigga. Hal already generated a fake email thread between us where Malechi asked me for more money promising to get the case dismissed while Tan did her accounting magic. Team work most definitely made the dream work.

"It's done," Malechi said as I checked my email for the paperwork. Once I saw it, I smiled because I already had Tan who also doubled as my secretary on standby to respond to him in a few hours demanding he call us or return our money.

"Wait Julian I have vital information that's worth you hearing you. I know who is-," he was saying but I was done listening to his snake ass.

"Nigga tell that shit to God since you bout to go see him cuz your services are no longer required," I said before putting a bullet between his eyes.

****

I woke up to the smell of breakfast cooking as I walked into the bathroom and handled my hygiene before going down the stairs to see Gabriela dancing around the kitchen cooking. Even though it was well after three am before I made it in this morning, her ass was still up hot and ready.

"I don't wanna play no games play no games, fuck about and give him my last name," she sang all loudly and off key as she danced around the kitchen.

The first day in our house, my momma woke up and came on our side of the house and cooked me breakfast even though she had her own kitchen and shit in her quarters. After Gabriela told her she wanted to cook for me from now own and could actually cook, ma didn't give her no shit about it which surprised the fuck out of me because she was big on cooking for her boys. Gabriela knew how to cook her ass off though and that's a trait I wasn't used to in a woman, but damn sure had grown to love.

She even knew how to cook Caribbean food and had hooked me up with a plate of rice and peas, and oxtails the other day that made me almost propose to her ass something I definitely said I wasn't doing. I loved her curly natural hair and her face without all of that makeup. She was extremely beautiful, and was glowing right now with her steady growing belly poking out. Walking up on her, I picked her up sitting her ass on the sink as I grabbed her by her throat and tongued kissed her. She had me doing everything out of my element because I damn sure wasn't with all that kissing shit but I loved the fuck out of her ass.

"Baby, ima burn the food I'm cooking for you," Gabriela said.

"Fuck that food, I'm tryna eat something else for breakfast," I said dropping down to my knees as I licked on her thighs pulling her to the edge of the sink until she was practically sitting on my face.

I didn't even bother taking her panties off, I just moved them to the side with my mouth as I began feasting on her pussy like a nigga was on death row. I still hasn't grown tired of this shit and would eat her pussy for breakfast, lunch, dinner, amid day snack, and everything in between.

"No Julian your mom," she said trying to run from me as I held on tighter.

"Knows after she caught me tearing your ass up on them stairs to call on the intercom before coming over here, now stop running from me," I growled at her as I took my thump sticking the tip of it inside of her giving her a double penetration.

"Fuck I can't take it," she said with her hands in my dreads trying to push my head back.

This only made me go harder causing her to get even wetter as I started French kissing her pussy jabbing my tongue in her shit mimicking exactly what my dick wanted to do. When I felt her legs shaking, I dropped my shorts before standing up pulling her face towards mines. I sloppily kissed her letting her taste all of her juices as I pushed inside of the warmest, tightest place on earth.

After I got done having my breakfast, I helped Gabriela clean up the kitchen, as I said,

"How does The Law Office of Gabriela Walters sound?"

"It sounds ok why you ask?"

"Because I had them put that on the front of the building already," I said tossing a set of keys her way. Her eyes got big as saucers once she saw them.

"Baby you didn't!" She said.

"Ain't that what you asked me for right? Oh yeah and that purse," I said.

"Yes but no one's ever done anything like this for me before. I've always wanted my own practice, and you just handed it to me," she said.

"Before you say something to unintentionally piss me off, let me stop you right there. I'm cut from a different cloth baby girl. As long as you show me you down to ride, be my peace when I need you to be, and hold shit down from your end, whatever you ask me to do ima make that shit happen. Besides ima always level my woman up, you fucking with a boss not a worker, so you damn sure won't be a worker. We own shit this way baby. I see your potential and I'm in love with your drive and your hustle," I said.

"I don't know what to say Julian! I love you, like I'm in love with you and I thought I would never love again. I thought I didn't deserve love, real love because of what I had allowed myself to settle for all those years. Then your rude ass came along and turned my peaceful world upside down. You've come into my life and literally changed it for the better in every way possible. I see things clearer and have such a different outlook on life, and I love it," she said walking up on me kissing me.

"Get your emotional big headed ass on," I said to her even though I felt the same way about her ass minus a bunch of that other shit she said.

Except I was too much of a G to keep getting all emotional with her ass. I allowed myself to break down one time and confess my feelings and that was enough for me.

"Come on get dressed so we can do see my new place of business. I can't wait to steal all of my clients back then go back to my old firm and throw it in those bitches faces," she said excitedly as I just shook my head at her.

"Family first fuck other clients," I said.

"Of course baby," she said. I didn't give a fuck about her old clients nor her old job, but we had to take care of Case first. We coming baby bro.

CREAM

"It's done," I said to the caller before hanging up the phone.

Taking a picture of the body in front of me chopped up and barely recognizable, I made sure I got a clear view of their damn face sending it off to my clients before I cleaned up and slipped out the house as casually as I had slipped in. I was a fucked up nigga from birth, so it's natural that I would live a fucked up life. Aside from out here in this streets with my boy L, I was a contract killer from a bunch of high profile muthafuckas. Shit not even L knew about this part of my life even though he knew I had a problem with killing muthafuckas. I honestly didn't know what it was about taking a life, but the shit was soothing to my ass.

With the life that I was born into, it's no surprise my ass grew up the way that I did. My pops used to whoop my mother's ass all day everyday but for no reason at all. He hated her ass so much that even her shadow pissed that nigga off. When beating her ass grew boring to him, he turned to me and my sisters and kid brother. The day I finally stood up to that nigga was the day I lost my family. Legend always thought I didn't know who my family was and was an orphan or some shit because I told him that, but I actually had a younger brother and two younger sisters. When Kevin Gates said to lose somebody you really love and they not dead, I felt that from the depths of my soul.

One day as usual my bitch ass daddy got to beating on everybody in the house, I'm talking about he used to beat us so badly that we had to miss school for days and weeks at a time until the bruises healed. Anyway, he had beat my mother so badly that she eventually passed out in a puddle of blood, and then he started on my little sisters and brother. He had beat my ass earlier but my mom had gotten him off of me that's how she ended up getting fucked up so badly. I had shook back though and something inside of me snapped. I decided today was the last day I was taken anymore ass whopping so I went inside the kitchen and got the biggest knife I could find then went looking for that nigga. I found him slapping my sister around as I yelled out to get his attention.

When he saw the knife in my hand, he actually laughed in my face. Asked me what I was gone do with that knife other than make him mad. I hadn't really thought that far as to what my ass planned on doing with it when I grabbed it. I was barely nine so to me it was gone be a scare tactic to get him out of the house. However, one minute he was coming towards me angrily, and the next, I had stabbed his ass in his neck and when he dropped to his knees, I had sliced his ass up about twelve time before his head hit the ground. I then cleaned everybody up. I knew by that point neighbors in the trailer parks we lived in had called the police by now.

Which they usually did and my momma would lie her way out of that nigga going to jail. Of course the murder weapon was still in the house so they took my ass to juvie that night. Two days later I had a hearing and everybody had to take the stand. I expected them all to tell the truth about him beating everybody ass and me killing him in self-defense. But these bitches got on the stand and acted like that piece of shit was father of the year! Even my mother fell out crying saying she didn't know why I would do something like that and my father loved me very much. The only thing that really saved my ass from doing a lot of time was the police reports they had on file about my neighbors reporting domestic violence, and all the time where we were forced to return to school early even if our bruises hadn't healed because we had already missed a lot of days.

They cut your government assistance if your kids weren't in school. I ended up still being sentenced to six years in a juvenile detention center because of how many times I had stabbed his ass. The judge called it over kill and thought maybe I had a mental problem. I did my time, hooked up with Legend, and haven't looked back since. I didn't care if them bitches were alive or what because they were dead to me.

*****

After I got home and got cleaned up, it was well after ten am and as tired as I am, I couldn't sleep for shit. I wasn't sure why I was restless lately, but I was. Between being in shoot outs, murkin' niggas with Legend, and doing my side business, a nigga definitely needed a goodnights rest. Didn't seem like today was the day I would get it though as I grabbed the keys to my Wrangler and headed out to door. I got in my Jeep and headed to Stacy's house. I'm not sure what is was that kept drawing me to her ass, but as hard as I tried to stay away, I found myself back in her space. It's been about two weeks since I last seen her ass. Two weeks since I stopped myself from killing her little ass. I was over her crib chilling as always because I don't let people in my personal space, so we was always at her crib. Anyway we had just matched a few blunts and was just talking and kickin' because she was actually cool to talk to. I felt like she understood where I was coming from on some real shit not on no fake ass lying to kick it type shit. Anyway, in the middle of us talking, her phone rang. I didn't think anything of it when she answered it and started talking because that wasn't my bitch so I didn't give a fuck what she did. I was on my phone scrolling through my emails picking and choosing which new job I wanted to take when she started giggling and shit all loud. Still, I let that shit slide because like I said that was her business. Anyway, when she said,

"Boy you crazy I do not be sounding like that." The shit kinda did something to me. I don't think it had anything to do with her talking to another nigga, and everything to do with the fact she did the shit in front of my face playing on my top and shit like I was some lil hoe ass nigga or something. I always thought because of my skin color niggas and bitches felt like they could play with me. Anyway, I told her hang that shit up and quit playing with me. She said some slick shit about that being her phone and I don't pay not one bill in her house so I couldn't tell her what to do with her shit.

Her mouth was so raw you would forget she was a bitch and bat her stupid ass up. I figured her bill couldn't have been no more than like $70 or some shit so I took a stack of money out, peeled a bill off and tossed it to her and told her hang the phone up. This bitch had the nerve to take that money, pocket it and say the bill for this month already been paid but she got me next month. I almost beat her fucking ass right there! I didn't, I did however take her phone out of her hand and broke that bitch! It wasn't the fact she was talking to that fuck nigga, it's the principal fuck she thought this shit was! She told me I was buying her a new phone and I told her ass to wait on it cuz I wasn't buying her ass shit! I knew she got a new phone because she texted me threatening me and cursing my ass out all last week. I left her dumb ass right on read even though I had been went cooped her ass the new iPhone 11 pro max, I didn't tell her ass that though. Even though I was headed to give it to her, this shit didn't mean any damn thing except I was replacing the weak ass phone I broke.

As I pulled up as her house, I saw another car in the drive way that I knew wasn't hers nor either of her friends. She only has two Destiny and Gabriela, and wouldn't let a random bitch be at her crib this early, so that left the only option being it belonged to a nigga. I pinched the bridge of my nose because this fucking girl right here was gone make me hurt her damn ass. I know I said I didn't give a fuck who she gave that pussy to, so I don't even know why I was bothered right now, but I was. Here I was talking about how L was acting with Gabriela but this bitch Stacy really had me all off my square and I really had to stop fucking with her. Making up my mind that I was gone hand her this weak ass phone and leave, I got out the car and went knocked on the door harder than I had to. A few minutes later a Chris brown reject looking ass nigga came to the door wearing nothing but some basketball shorts.

"Say my man what can I do for you," his ass said sizing me up and down seeing that I was white and quickly dismissing me.

What he did that for I didn't know because that just made the animal in me come out as my disrespectful side flared up.

"You can't do shit for me my nigga," I said hoeing his ass as I invited myself in pushing past him.

"Who at the door Johnathan?" I heard Stacy yell from the kitchen as I casually strolled in her shit and took a seat at the kitchen table.

"Shit smells good ma hook me up with a plate," my stupid ass said staring at how her ass was eating the shorts she had on up.

You would have thought she saw a ghost how she turned around looking at me when I said that.

"Who the fuck is this lame ass Eminem, Malibu's Most Wanted ass nigga Stacy?"

Dude said just making it to the kitchen. When I walked past him and he didn't get off on my ass, I knew then that he was pussy. Win, lose, or draw, ain't no nigga gone hoe me.

"The nigga that stay in them guts rearranging them walls," I said looking at her the entire time I said this as I watched her body react to my words just as I knew it would.

Her mouth won't say it, but her body knew what it was hitting for with me. I was a cocky nigga with a big dick and I knew it. I definitely didn't fit into no lying ass stereotypes; I was a different bred in my own league.

"Cream what are you doing in my shit?" Stacy said finally getting her voice back.

"Nigga? You ain't black bitch you little fake ass Justin Bieber. And that's what you be doing? Re arranging them guts? That's funny me and you be doing the same thing huh," Johnathan said which instantly pissed me off and I didn't even know why.

I tried to shake it off but it was too late, I wanted blood.

"You giving this nigga my pussy Stacy?"

"Huh? Your pussy? The one attached to my body?" She said.

"If she was what you gone do about it bitch boy?" Dude said walking closer to me that I would have liked.

Nigga looked like Terry Crews like he lived in the gym all day every day, but I wasn't bothered as I remained calm.

"Send this nigga home Stacy and fix me a plate before I get mad and you see me show my ass," I said giving her a choice which is something I never did.

I was slightly amused to see which option she could go with.

"Show yo ass then nigga," dude said.

"Cream this is my house, I don't be blowing your spot up now do I? Normal people call and wait to be invited over," she said.

"That's how you feel?" I asked her for clarity.

"That's what she said ain't it." Dude said as I assessed the situation for a second.

I had come over here with a peace offering some shit I never did, intending to try and make amends for my actions the last time. I walk in here and her ass giving my pussy away, pussy I just beat down two weeks ago. On top on that taking up for this bitch ass body builder ass nigga. Both of them really had me fucked up right now. I closed my eyes as I again repeated myself.

"Stacy send this nigga home so we can talk," I said.

"Bitch ass nigga you put me out then if you want me to go," Dude voice said slicing though my tranquility I was trying to build for myself.

At this point he was standing directly over me as I was seated. My eyes shot open as I grabbed the fork that was on her table that she usually kept set already with fancy plates, knife and forks. Anyway, I grabbed the fork jumping up as I stabbed his ass in the neck quickly about five damn times with precision knowing exactly which arteries to hit.

"Put you out? Cool only way you leaving is a body bag though," I said as I stabbed him once more as blood squirted everywhere and Stacy screamed.

"Naw where that tough girl act just went? Shut the fuck up before you join this nigga. I came here to give you a peace offering and you tried to play me. In here with your ass out giving this nigga my pussy then tried to hoe me! His death on your hands! Let that nigga be a constant reminder the next time to try that bullshit," I barked as I pulled my phone out calling the cleanup crew.

*****

"Nigga yo ass out here fucking wilding my G!" Legend said as soon as he walked in the warehouse.

I was on blunt number three trying to calm my nerves. I had already texted and told him what happened and I'm sure Stacy called Gabriela.

"You would have done the same thing had that been Gabriela," I

said.

"Yeah because that's my lady, you still claim you don't fuck with Stacy like that," he said.

"Shit I don't it's the fucking principal of the matter. I don't give a fuck how much we just cool, don't disrespect me in front of another nigga!" I said.

"Nigga you wasn't even supposed to be there! You just popped up so how was you disrespected? And which part was disrespectful? The part where the nigga was there? Of the fact that the nigga was there with Stacy the bitch you in denial about liking," he said.

"Nigga why you in yo chest? Doing all this damn yelling!" I said jumping up.

"Because I got enough shit on my plate with my own shit, and Case shit. I don't need to add your shit to it. You doing dumb shit like murking muthafuckas in broad daylight in front of people is sloppy as fuck," he said.
 I murk people in daylight every day, I thought to myself.

"Man fuck that bitch! On me I'm done with that hoe. The streets can have her," I said getting up fixing me a drink meaning every word I said.

Anything that complicated or added stress to my already fucked up life had to go. Shit Stacy was ghetto and loud, but she used to be somebody I could unwind from a long day with. That shit was dead now fuck that bitch!

STACY

Smoking another blunt, I tried to calm my nerves as the men cleaned my kitchen from top to bottom. When they were finished, you would swear you and down no way a murder had just occurred. But I couldn't get the image of Johnathan's lifeless body out of my head if I wanted to. The sickest part about everything was the fact Cream made me watch as they chopped Johnathan's body into pieces disposing of it into separate contains.

All the reason I chased hard after Cream were the same reason I now felt like I wanted to run far and fast away from his ass. What was most intriguing about him was the fact he said he saw me, so I didn't have to try hard to make him see me. I didn't really get it until he broke it down for me, letting me know that I was a person who oozed sex appeal and was beautiful and expected men to fall at my feet basically and chase me; which I did because their asses did. Cream said I did this because I had a walk up and instead of offering somebody my heart, I offered them my looks and my body instead. For somebody I never normally went for, he was the only guy that ever saw through to the real me making him even more desirable to me.

But, shit even after me letting my guard down with me being myself, kicking it with him smoking a blunt and revealing real shit about myself; I still was the old me. Shit he was still a hoe and slanging dick like it was going out of style so I was still using these niggas as well, the fuck. I liked to consider myself the female version of a nigga, I didn't love these niggas, and I would trick them out they head, and then send them home to their bitch when I was done. I was untamable with everybody else Cream because he actually humbled my mean ass. Still, he couldn't expect me to give all of me when he only gave me 30% of himself in return. Sure we got real in our talks we had, but not that damn real because as much as he told me, I still didn't know much about him. And it hasn't slipped past me the fact that I've never been to this man crib, and don't even know where it's to begin with. Yet his ass popping up at my shit like he pays bills in this bitch wilding like that! Like the most I thought about it, the more fucked up I realized he had me!

Knock! Knock!

I got up to open the door as I saw Destiny and Gabriela's pregnant ass standing there. I already had my purse and keys in my hand and had changed into some clothes as I locked my door and headed to the car. I wanted to sit and talk anywhere but that damn house even though it was back spotless. I had worked my ass off to buy that house! It wasn't much but it was mines, now I might put it up for sale because Cream had ruined the peace I felt every time I came home.

*****

"As much as you and Destiny preached to me about the do's and don'ts of dealing with somebody like Legend, I can't believe you didn't take your own advice Stacy. I mean Cream's weird ass gives a new meaning to the word crazy because he is beyond that," Gabriela said.

"Bitch you been getting hit with some trap nigga dick all of a few months and suddenly you an expert," I said playfully as I burst out laughing.

"Almost seven months to be exact and yes that definitely makes me a damn expert because even I'm not that damn crazy," she said.

"I'm with Gabriela on this one Stacy why you tried that light skinned muthafucka like he wasn't with the shits?" Destiny said

"Because that was my shit! He not my nigga, we ain't even like that, we just chill, smoke, and fuck that's it! He can't come in my shit I pay bills at demanding I put my company out!" I said yelling louder than I intended to but nobody seemed to get I was not in the fucking wrong in this situation! That crazy ass nigga was.

"No bitch your problem is you used to walking all over niggas because they let your ass. They don't say shit if you fuck one and kick them out for another one, but you should have known you couldn't try that shit with Cream! He told Julian about how you called some dude in from of him a few weeks back in his face. I've been at your house before when you would have a guy over and literally be on the phone with another guy like he wasn't there. You have this point to prove that nobody can tell you what to do or some shit but you met your match in Cream," Gabriela said putting me in my place for the first time in our friendship.

I had to have been fucking up if that bitch could tell me about myself.

"Niggas do it all the time so why can't I? Shit a nigga can't handle when you pull a them on they asses! They play women all the time but when you play them first they get in their little feelings! Miss me with that shit! This why I'll always rally for Amber Rose Slut Walk movement," I stubbornly said folding my arms together.

"Bitch I'm all for not being a damn fool for a nigga, but everything you describing, has that happened to you with Cream? Has he called a bitch in front of you and held a conversation with the hoe?" Destiny said as I thought about it.

His phone always rang off the hook when we chilled but he

would just look at it and silence it.

"His hoes stay calling him I see the shit, he'll silence the phone though on some slick shit," I said.

"But the keyword is silence! He silenced the call, you answered it!" Gabriela said.

"Bitch fuck that nigga I ain't never rode this hard for somebody over you! You supposed to be on my side right or wrong."

"I'm always on your side! That will never change but don't always call me out on my shit then get mad when the tables turn. I don't give a fuck about Cream; I'm telling you as your friend you wrong! You were disrespectful regardless of the fact if he was invited or not. It was bad enough you were throwing the fact you just slept with another guy in his face, but then you taunted him when he still tried to be the bigger person. You dead ass wrong," Gabriela said not backing down and shutting my ass down yet again.

I knew all of this was true but yet I still tested Cream anyway knowing he wouldn't let me do him like others guys. But, my stubborn ass still told myself I didn't give a fuck who he was! I was on my Megan thee Stallion shit when she said *handle me? Who gone handle me?* I felt like I could treat everybody the same, and today taught me I was merely gambling with my life.

"I hadn't just slept with him," I finally admitted.

"Ok bitch well you fucked him that night same difference," Destiny said.

"No I'm on my period, I haven't fucked anybody since Cream," I said.

"Why you let them think that's what happened then?" Gabriela said

"Because that nigga don't run shit this way," my stubborn ass

said.

"You gone lose that nigga watch! Yo ass lying to yo self-knowing you'll be sick if he start giving another bitch the dick you been getting," Destiny said.

"I can't lose something that was never mines to begin with," I said trying to sound nonchalant, but the thought of him fucking another bitch and giving her the time and attention he gave me hurt more than I expected it to no matter how hard I acted.

"Every night before a few weeks ago if he wasn't out with Julian handing business he was at your house right? Ain't no man like Cream spending that much time with somebody if he doesn't like them. Both of y'all stubborn, you just stubborn and disrespectful," Gabriela said.

"I'm telling though, you give this bitch some good dick one time and she turn into Dr. Phil and shit," Destiny said.

"Right! This bitch toe the fuck up," I said as well fell out laughing.

Once we stopped it grew silent for a while until Gabriela spoke up,

"Do you like him Stacy? Like really like him like him?"

It took me awhile to answer that question because I had to really reach deep within and ask myself that question. Like past the wall I put up and lies I automatically had programmed inside of myself as a defense mechanism. Did I actually honestly really like Cream? Realization set in before my mouth formed the answer as I nodded my head yes.

"I might have lost him forever though because he told me he would never fuck with me again before he left out the house," I said.

"Girl you know as well as I do that nigga just in his chest talking!

Destiny said.

"If you really like him ima give you the same advice you gave me, stop playing and get you man before another bitch do," Gabriela said. I heard what they were saying but as I really say back and replayed everything in my mind that had happened and the part I played in it, I knew that was easier said than done.

****

It had been a few days since everything had happened and tonight Gabriela had invited me over to the house for dinner and bowling at their house. She had convinced Legend somehow to get Cream to show up even after he told her ass to mind her own business.

That my was bitch so I knew she was gone make it happen. She had that nigga wrapped around her finger and didn't even know it. Cream had blocked my ass on everything, so this was my one chance to make amends. Looking myself over in the mirror one more time, I admired my outfit making sure I looked good. I was wearing a long sleeve powder pink turtle neck crop top, with high waisted ripped up distress Bermuda shorts that stopped above my knees. I had gotten the shorts from fashion nova and they made my waist look snatched and had my ass literally sitting up. Beyoncé's felling myself played in my head as I grabbed my stuff and headed out the door satisfied with everything.

Following the directions Gabriela had told me, I pulled up into what looked like the woods as I thought maybe my GPS was fucked up. However, when I went to pull my phone up, I realized I somehow had suddenly lost the four bars I knew I just had!

"What the fuck!" I said frustrated that I was about to have to turn around and head back the other way until I got signal to only turn around and drive back this way. I put my car in reverse as I saw a car whip into the woods behind me. I immediately grabbed my gun I kept under my seat as the car pulled up beside me and put their car in park. I say there debating to drive off, start shooting or what before the window rolled down and I saw that it was Cream.

"Why the fuck," I started as he cut me off.

"Look I told sis I would let you ride in with me so come the fuck on and cut the questions," he said coldly to me.

"Giving up the losing battle, I kept my gun as I grabbed everything else I needed, locked my car up and got in his car. When he noticed my gun still out he smirked.

"You could be taking me into the woods to murder me or something nigga," I said.

"I would have left your brains on the flood beside that bitch nigga that same day if I wanted you dead," was all he said as he put his car in drive and drove through the woods.
I put the safety on and put the gun in my purse. After he drove through, instead of seeing more trees and shit, it actually turned out to be a little dirt road instead that went on and own for about five minutes before we came to a huge gate and a booth with a guard in it. When he saw Cream, he waved him in pressing a button as the gate swung open revealing yet another dirt road.

"Where the fuck we going," I said as my voice trailed off as the biggest house I had ever seen in my life suddenly came into view. The shit was like one of those castles on every princess fairy tale movie except this shit was really here, and my bitch was living it. Instead of feeling jealousy, I was immediately happy thinking **that's my muthafuckin dawg! Bitch you betta!**

"What you was just saying?" Cream smirked putting his car in park.

"I didn't have sex with him," I blurted out. I felt like was now or never to get that out. When he didn't say anything I continued talking. "I mean I have had sex with him before, but my period was that day."

"So your period being in the only reason the nigga ain't smash huh?" He smirked throwing me for a loop before I wasn't expecting that response.

"What? Huh? That's not what I'm saying. I'm saying. I haven't had sex anyone since we last had sex two weeks ago." I said.

"Because your period was on, I heard you," he coldly said getting out.

"What about you Cream! Hold yourself to that same standard!" I said to his back because he had already gotten out the car and closed the door. Feeling defeated, I got out the car and followed him to the front door, his ass didn't even knock, just walked in. When I say when I stepped inside, I felt like I walked into one of them houses off cribs or some shit I was not lying. Everything we passed was gorgeous as we kept waking until we came to a living room. I saw Legend as he dapped Cream up before saying to me,

"Gabriela in the kitchen with my momma cooking," as he pointed in the direction of the kitchen.

I walked in as she was standing over the stove stirring the pot and laughing with who I assumed was Legends mother. When she noticed me, she said something to her future mother in Jamaican and came where I was.
"Well?" She asked me.

"Well what bitch? I mean girl," I said forgetting that fast his momma was in the kitchen with us.

"What happened on the ride over here with Cream?"

"My phone doesn't work out here or I would have called and cursed you out," I said pulled my phone out to show her but surprisingly I had four bars now.

"What the hell?" I said.

"Ignore that, now spill the beans hoe," she said like it was something normal that always happened.

"Well bitch let's just say I was sitting in that car feeling how Yvette off Baby Boy felt while sitting at that table and Jody just ignored her and kept playing cards. So, she ran outside crying talking about he don't love me no more, get me out of here," I said as Gabriela burst out laughing but I was dead as serious.

Cream acted so cold towards me that I was ready to tuck my tail between my legs, and leave with the little bit of dignity I still had left. Especially when he tossed that question at me. It threw me for a loop because had I not been on my period I probably would have given Johnathan some ass but how does that make me the bad person?

"I'm for real like he doing me bad like I just really did something to him when really this nigga out here slanging dick just left and right, shit the streets be talking. I was in the nail shop minding my own business one day when I heard his name being brought up. I knew they was talking about his ass I knew it was him cus what other Cream that's out here gettin serious paper and crazy? Anyway the bitch was talking about how he crazy but fucked her into a coma and she ain't expect him to come like that. When she said that it's like three or four other hoes all had stories about being fucked by this nigga on some sista wives type shit, but I'm the bad guy?" I said.

"Bitch you can't play these get back games, you smart enough to know that. But, he just still mad, but I'm positive he not done with your ass. I'm sure you're just in time out," Gabriela said confidently.

"How you figure?"

"Because when I told him to wait on you and y'all ride in together, he didn't put up a fuss at all," she said.

"Bitch that's because you asked him, I'm sure he was talking shit, just not to you," said again forgetting to watch my mouth.

"Trust me if he objected he would have most definitely told me and Julian, Cream's crazy ass doesn't care who he curses out," she said.

I hated to admit it, but hearing that gave me a tad bit of hope. Shit I needed everything I could get at this point with this stubborn ass nigga.

*****

Two hours later we found ourselves in Gabriela and Legends game room where Cream was treating me even worse than before. It's like after I told him I was on my period, and that's why I didn't fuck Johnathan, that nigga became even more done with my ass. He completely ignored me at dinner and talked around me like I wasn't even there. Then we went to their bowling alley, and instead of playing on teams with me, he cut up so badly that it had to be me and Gabriela against him and Legend.

To top it all off, a bitch Face Timed him and he answered it and this hoe was loudly telling him how she wanted to suck his dick and all this. When he told her have that pussy freshly shaved and waiting for him because he'll be over soon to bring her that dick, I was done. Fuck him this why I play niggas now because soon as you give them the power to hurt you, they show their asses. Gabriela and Legends freaky ass damn near almost started fucking on the bowling alley floor. My girl went from scared of dick damn near to throwing it back like a champ for a real nigga. After Legends ass literally damn near fucked her with us in the room, they finally left me and Cream and went to do their own thing.

Well they left me because Cream was still on FaceTime with a bitch. I was completely over the situation as I got up to go in search of a bathroom even though it was one in the bowling alley because this room legit put you in the mind of a real bowling alley. It even had a concession stand and few vending machines. I really just wanted to get away from Cream before I hauled off and hit his stupid disrespectful ass. I'm mad I rode here with him but how I was feeling, I might take off walking back to my car. Walking off down the hallway, I started exploring this huge ass castle that was just ridiculously big. Opening a door, I stumbled upon an indoor basketball court as the tomboy in me that played ball in high school came out. Picking a basketball out from the rack lined against the wall, as I dribbled and shot a few rounds. The lights suddenly went out as I looked around thinking maybe they were on a timer or some shit. I wouldn't put it past this big ass house. So, after I tried to find a light switch and couldn't, I used my phone to gather all my shit together and left out. Trying to remember which hallway I walked down, I made a right and a left trying to get back to the bowling alley because I was more than ready to go home. Getting a text on my phone, I looked down to reply when I felt a hand go over my mouth as I was lifted off my feet and pulled into a dark room. My first reaction was to start swinging wildly as I felt myself being pushed against a wall. So many crazy ass thoughts went through my mind as I heard,

"Ain't no fun when the rabbit's got the gun now is it?" Cream said as I felt something slide down my pants before he took one hand and physically pulled them apart.

"What the fuck are you talking about Cream? And did you just cut my damn pants off me you crazy ass muthafucka I paid $45 for these," I said attempting to push him off me so I could turn around and swing on his ass!

"You know my pockets different from them other clowns you fuck with, I'll pay for it," he said before sliding my thong to the side and pushing his dick so deep inside of me it made me stand up on my tiptoes trying to crawl up the wall damn near.

I wouldn't say he was always gentle with me in the past, but he wasn't this damn ruthless.

"You was mad as fuck when you saw me on the phone huh?" He said roughly fucking me against the wall. It hurt so badly but it also felt so good as I started throwing my ass back at him.

"Oh you like that bitch?" He said roughly wrapping his fingers in my hair yanking it hard as he could taking one of my legs propping it up on something, dipping down low going even deeper inside of me at a fast as quick paste. All you heard in the room was skin slapping as I tried not to give him the satisfaction of screaming out because I knew at this point he was trying to hurt me.

"Why you wanna play with me Stacy? You was gone give my shit away? That's what you was gone do? But got mad that a bitch wanna swallow this dick huh?"
He said in my ear before biting me on the side of my neck then sucking really hard on that spot marking his territory.

When he reached his hand around my body and started playing with my pussy, I lost the tough guy act as I started moaning loud as hell. He was fucking my entire life up and I was loving every moment of it.

"I'm sorry baby I promise it won't happen again ," I screamed shit I would promise him the stars, moon, the sky, my social security number, shit I'll talk a charge right now if he asked me. Long as he kept fucking me like this. Right when I felt myself on the verge of exploding, he suddenly pulled out of me. Turning around, I was breathing hard as hell looking him up and down thinking how I could beat his ass.

"Yo ass mad huh? You mad I took this dick away from you?" He said taunting me as I hauled off and tried to hit him as he grabbed both of my arms pinning me against the wall.

"That nigga death on your head, I ain't a nigga you can play games with Stacy. That'll be the outcome every time you think you gone play with me. I'ma fucked up individual who had a fucked up life, so that will always be my reaction to bullshit. You either gone get your shit together, or you gone be stuck crying in the car like Yvette while another bitch pick up your slack?" His said as my cheeks burned red because his ass had heard me. I guess I was taking too long to answer him because he started pulling his pants up before I quickly reached out stopping his movements. Dropping to me knees, before I sucked the soul out of his dick, I decided to do something I've been afraid all my life of doing as I put my faith in my nigga for the first time.

"Ima get my shit together baby," I said before spitting on his dick taking him deep into my mouth happily. I couldn't believe how things had quickly turned around for me. Came for the food, leaving with my man.

CASE

"**9**8, 99,100," I said as I sat the weights down and sat up grabbing the towel wiping sweat off my face. That's all I've pretty much been doing since I got in this bitch, fighting and hitting that iron. It wasn't shit else for me to do. I damn sure couldn't sit around stressing about something I couldn't control. I knew L thought I was careless and out there in the streets wilding out, so that's how I got locked up. But, that shit was far from the truth.

Yeah I stunted on niggas and I'm flashy sometimes, but I'm a young paid ass nigga getting big boy money so that's to be expected. I'm barely twenty running a multimillion dollar empire. Sure ever since my brother started seeing money he always threw me bread. But, it's a difference between somebody buying you a car, clothes and throwing you a couple thousand, then you doing that shit yourself and touching a couple million dollars. I literally touched my first million within six months of L turning everything over to me and that shit was a feeling I will never fully be able to explain. So yeah, I was flashy, but I damn sure wasn't reckless.

I knew how high the stakes were just like I knew how important this job was. Filling the infamous Legend's shoes was a big task, but I feel like I rose to the challenge. Shit more comes with that shit than niggas think, even my brother didn't understand what that really means. It ain't easy to even be a great value version of him, so it was definitely harder being his kid brother. People expected us to operate the same, think the same, move the same, and even fuck with people the same. But, I had my own fucking mind, and did shit my own fucking way. With Legend, before he made a move, 1+ 1 had to perfectly equal 2 just by adding 1. However, with me, I didn't give a fuck what corners I had to cut, and didn't give a fuck if something had to be added, divided or subtracted. If we both arrived at the same number of 2 then what difference does it make the separate routes we each took to get to it? Shit didn't run smoothly in my world and that was the beauty of it because I didn't want it to. Still, regardless of my crazy methods, I wasn't sloppy with big transactions, didn't take any and everybody as a new client, nor was I reckless enough to end up on the FBI radar. No way they had been watching me because if they had been, they would have got me on way more shit than the drugs I been caught with since I had my hands in a little bit of everything. None of which my brother knew about. So, the shit wasn't making sense and I had been asking my snake ass lawyer for a while now to get me my paperwork. They couldn't deny him the fucking paperwork they had on me saying they had me under surveillance x amount of days, months, or years. But I have yet to hear anything from that nigga Malechi concerning shit dealing with my case. Actually, each time he talked to my ass, it's never about these charges and what he gone do to get me a bond. The goofy ass nigga always on some extra snake ass shit asking me about transaction dates, drop off locations, and who all I supply to.

Talking about some its relevant to this case that I tell him the information. Nigga was playing on my top thinking because I'm young I'm stupid or some shit. I know the feds don't give a fuck about who I supply, and where because to them I'm a big fish, their goal is to take me down. They don't give a fuck about nobody if they not a bigger fish than me. I ain't told L my suspicions about this nigga just yet because I want his ass to slip up and tell me some shit that will let me know his motive and who sent his bitch ass. Malechi had me confused with some sucker ass clown ass nigga. The more he talked, the further he talked himself into some shit that's why I was keeping my eyes on him. Shit he ain't the only one I'm keeping my eyes on though because I got a funny feeling somebody in my crew turnt snitch, but I don't know who. Contrary to what my brother thinks, I would never play around with the large number of drugs I was getting from that nigga Silas.

I already knew what type of nigga he was, and knew we would have to take it there if he was even a fucking $1 short! So, I never took the same route twice, and nobody but the crew set to go that day with me knew the route for that re up. So, either the Feds was really watching Silas and busted me, or one of my niggas gave the routes up. They did right by separating us though because I definitely would have gotten to the bottom of the shit by now. Looking around as I got up and walked back to my cell, I did what I did best, what my brother taught me to do; analyzed my surroundings. I knew who was really living like that, and what snitching ass niggas was living on borrowed time and didn't even know it. Shit that was half the niggas in this bitch though and they asses always had a damn excuse as to why they snitched. *"I got kids to think about."* *"My momma sick,"* *" I'm all my peoples got."* Niggas be having more excuses than a lying ass green dot working ass nigga trying to explain how he can turn your $50 into $500. Bottom line is, in the free world, all that rah rah bullshit sounds good until them pigs cased your ass up and get to talking football numbers unless you turn snitch. That's when the real bitch in a lot of niggas came out! As young as I was, and as much as I didn't want to be here, I was ready for this shit! I knew what came with it before I jumped off the porch. I never had a daddy that I can remember, so L taught me all I know and made sure I didn't fear shit but God. That's why as much as I prayed I didn't have to, if push came to shove and I had to lay it down for a few years it was what it was, I was prepared to do that.

****

Walking back towards my cell, I immediately knew something wasn't right the second I walked up to that bitch. For one, it was strangely quiet, when usually bitch ass corrections officers always harassing muthafuckas about coming back to their cell early. Everything in this bitch worked on a time schedule and no matter if you wanted to do the shit or not, everybody gotta stick to the schedule. Well there was them, and then there was my ass. I didn't follow nan nigga rules on the street, so those same rule applied in jail. I always got into fights with the guards on Tuesday's, because Tuesday's were the days I was in population outside with everybody else. However, I usually got my workout in, then headed back in to hit the showers first and relax with a book or some shit. Just because I was a thug didn't mean I was dumb and couldn't read. Anyway, being alert like my brother raised me, shit seemed fishy to me. Instead of turning back around and going back the way I had just come, I however walked into my cell, and grabbed clothes to hit the showers anyway. If ever it was a time where my life was threatened, I damn sure wasn't going out like no bitch hiding behind guards and other inmates and shit. Like my big brothers always told me,

"Case when you find yourself outnumbered and you know that's it for you, you make them muthafuckas work for your life." So fearlessly, I held my head up high and kept alert and on guard as I headed towards the showers. Being that I was waiting for them niggas to go with their move, I heard the big slew footed ass nigga running up on me before he was anywhere near me as I discreetly slipped my shank out of my shorts that I kept there at all times. Legend had taught me how to box, and how to anticipate my opponent, so I waited until I sensed he was close enough up on me before I turned around and quickly went in for the kill stabbing that niggas about nine times before he knew what hit him. The funny thing was, when I turned around, the nigga had his hand up with his shank in it just about to poke my stupid ass

up.

"The nigga who sent your stupid ass on this duck mission should have told you that you gotta be quicker than that lil bitch," I said as he dropped to his knees.

Not one to risk a nigga surviving and coming back for revenge, I bent down and stabbed his ass a few more times to make sure he was dead. I looked around making sure nobody saw me as I quickly made my way to the shower washing my shank off and then stashing it somewhere. I knew I wouldn't make it back to my cell with that bitch and I damn sure wasn't about to get no murder charge added to me. Soon as I had stashed the shank, I heard the code red sirens going off and madness flooded the jail. Them niggas were just nowhere to be found when it was an attempted murder on my life, but code red and they ass came running. I wonder if they thought that it was me taking my last breath on that floor? Bitches gone be mad when they see it's not. I quickly washed up because I knew they was about to be in here any minute now beating my ass because I was in here showering.

***

"Mr. Santiago, why must we go through this with you every Tuesday?" The warden said.

After like six niggas beat my ass, they sent me to the infirmary to patch me up and then sent me to see the warden.

"Shit we don't have to, I don't be fucking with y'all, y'all be fucking with a nigga," I said.

"You have this cocky ass nonchalant attitude now because you have a case that's still pending. Mark my words, as soon as the judge says guilty, that ass is mines. I bet you straight up then," he said.

"That ass is yours? Ole fruity ass nigga you can miss me with that gay shit. And shit when the judge says guilty, won't shit change unless free time moves to Wednesday," I said as he grabbed me up by my orange jumpsuit slamming me against his office wall just as his phone began to ring interrupting whatever he was about to do.

I smirked as it continued to ring.

"My line stay blowing up with my hoes calling, but that call for you warden," I said fucking with him.

Nigga was madder than a bitch as he angrily let me go and picked up the phone.

"Hello?" He said as his face frowned up.

"He did what? That's impossible check it again." He paused.

"I'm telling you he didn't have one so that has to be a computer error. I personally checked on it so check it again."
"His who? What lawyer? I talked to-wait who is that? Where the other lawyer at?" He said.

Clearly this nigga was upset about something and the entire time he kept looking at me making my antennas stand up. He hung up as he came over and looked at me as his whole face was slowing turning beet red. That nigga looked like he wanted to beat my ass as he raised his fist to hit me at the same time as the door to his office burst open.

"You touch my client and I'll tie this fucking prison up in so many damn lawsuits you'll be lucky to get a job as a flash light cop when I'm done with your ass," I heard looking over his shoulders as my eyes landed on Gabriela.

"You my lawyer now sis?"

"Yeah let's get go, you were processed out over two hours ago! Had me waiting all this damn time, oh I got something for y'all asses tomorrow though," her ass said still going off.

I sent a prayer up to the man above for sending her ass to my brother as I happily bumped the warden as I walked past him.

I damn sure wasn't expecting this when I opened my eyes this morning, shit I thought I would never get a bond, so I was happy as hell right now. This must be the surprise Legend was telling me about. They done really fucked up by freeing a real nigga. I was officially about to touch down and cause hell.

*****

"Man why you ain't been home to see ya girl yet? Got Dana's bald headed ass was blowing my fucking phone up all last night had my girl going up side my head thinking that bitch was for me. I don't know how her ass even found out you was free. I wanted this shit to be kept on the low for now," Legend said as I opened the door to my penthouse suite that I was holed up in.

"Man maybe she called my cellphone and that bitch ass CO told her I was out or some shit. I don't know, I got business to handle though. So as much as I want to, I can't be laid up in no pussy right now," I said truthfully. I hope L didn't think I was gone come home and hide out on some bitch shit and continue letting him handle my baggage for me. If so, it wasn't no need for him to have had sis get my ass out just to play hide and seek with niggas.
"Look at my nigga growing up on me and shit but nigga where the fuck you get a suit from? Where you going?" He asked me pointing to the suit I had hanging up that I had picked up earlier.

"We gone get into that in a second, first how you ended up firing Malachi's ass and having sis take over?"

"Nigga I canceled that bitch ass nigga; I didn't fire shit. He technically ran off with my money and I had to file all types of charges against his law office and bar number," he said before giving me the run down on what actually happened.

"Damn I ain't want you to pop that nigga yet," I said telling him what I had been keeping from him. He got this look in his eyes as he said,

"Damn that's probably what that nigga was talking about. Before I popped his ass he was tryna plea bargain and tell me he knew some vital information," He said.

"Shit whatever it is the shit gone come out sooner rather than later."

"I'm ready for whatever shit you already know this. Back to this damn suit though, you finna going apply for a job or some shit?"

"Nigga what the fuck I look like punching somebody damn clock? That shit ain't even me, and I'll never be that nigga I don't give a fuck what a judge or whoever ordered me to do. But, this suit part of the real reason why I called you over here. You may not agree with it, but ima stand on all ten like a man. This my shit that I got you into, and ima get you out of it. It's time for me to take responsibility for my actions," I said.

"Nigga you know what type of charges you just came home on? You ass need to sit the fuck down somewhere," he said.

"Nigga if you wanted me to sit the fuck down, you should have left my ass sitting down in jail. Now that I'm up, I got moves to make. I'm not gone try and take back over right now, shit but I do need to make amends with this war I started and make sure my men eating properly," I said.

"What that mean? Shit I opened shop back up, they eating just fine" he said.

"Yeah but for how long? The secret stash won't last forever, I got this. This suit for a sit down, and I want you Cream and Jaxson to roll with me," I said. Jaxson was a little nigga I had vetted before I left. The nigga was fearless and had more heart than niggas twice his age.

"Ok who we having a sit down with a possible new plug?"

"Naw ima go sit down face to face and look the devil in his eyes."

****

"Yo we all looking cleaner than a bitch right now," I said because we all had suits on even Cream's crazy ass.

"The first sign that this nigga on bullshit, I'm shooting that shit up," Legend said he was beyond pissed finding out I called Silas and asked to come politic with him.

Shit I'm man enough to admit I'm in the wrong in this situation even though it's not my fault what happened. If a nigga get jacked with my drugs I'm not gone understand it not being his fault, ima want my bread, simple. Legend on the other hand was so mad, he made me square up with his ass, then the nigga pistol whipped my ass. I think that's partially because he knew like I knew this shit was on me however he wanted to spin it; this was my fuck up. This the reason niggas pockets getting fucked up, and why Legend had to step back in a position he damn sure didn't want to. But regardless and no matter what, as my big brother he was always trying to fight my battles for me. Not this time, if this sit down ain't work and Silas wanted to take it there, well then I was ready for that. I had the connections for that. I ain't have shit but time on my hands to be playing these life for a life games with this nigga. I loved that Wild Wild West. L on the other hand was happily legit, and retired, and now he got a kid on the way. This wasn't his battle and I wanted that made clear today.

"I'm letting y'all know now, this muthafucka done tried me on levels other muthafuckas wouldn't even dare reach. He threatened my seed talking about he'll take everything I never got to love, he tried to burn ma up in her house, then the nigga sent his men at us in a crazy ass shoot out. So, if this bitch breaths wrong, I'm airing this muthafucka out," Legend said.

"Shit you know soon as you up that tool I'm going with my move too. If you rocking, I'm rolling, "Cream said.

"Shit I stay locked and loaded," Jaxson added.

"All y'all niggas chill out. This a grown man sit down, ain't none of that shit going on," I said trying to be the voice of reason. Me, the usual hot head was trying to be on some grown man shit.

"Keep thinking that," L said as the car came to a stop.

One by one we all hopped out that bitch looking like we was about to audition for making the band or some shit how we were all color coordinated and shit. Everybody even all had a pair of black Ray Bans on but nobody planned this shit. Grabbing my briefcase, we all headed across the street to the Chinese restaurant. As soon as Legend opened the door, two big beefy niggas started walking up on us.

"Don't even play yourself," I said as the one closest to me attempted to grab my briefcase.

"Shit don't look this way either nigga, they know me in this bitch, better ask them about what happened to the last nigga who tried that bullshit," Legend said as Cream and Jaxson both stood their silent but looking deadly as fuck.

They were apart in age, that's it because them two niggas acted just alike.

"Let them pass," we all heard as the top flight security niggas just smirked and moved out the way as we walked into the empty restaurant that only had one customer sitting at a table alone eating. Walking up to his table, me and L both pulled out a chair and had a seat as Cream and Jaxson slide in a booth behind us. Meanwhile, the nigga sitting in front of us eating never looked up from the plate of food he was fucking over. When he was done, he wiped his hands and mouth, and picked his beer up taking a gulp from it before finally looking up acknowledging us.

"Case, it's nice to see you looking good. I see you didn't get turnt into nobody's bitch while doing time," he said.

"Shit it don't matter how fuckin' long I would have or still gotta do, that shit wouldn't' have never happened. Bodies would have started to pile up," I said.

"Let's take this conversation to the back," he said.
"Shit ain't nobody here, so why we can't talk now? This ain't no damn social call bruh, you know exactly why we here," my brother said agitated at this point. He had short patience and bad nerves and this nigga knew that so I didn't know why he was sitting in our face playing these fuck ass games.

"Big bad Legend you still haven't figured out you not invincible?"

"Bitch ass Silas, you still haven't figured out you not Casper? Yet you stay disappearing and sending bitch niggas to fight for you when shit gets real. Meanwhile I'm always on the battlefield ready for whatever," Legend said.

"And for the last fucking time I ain't got to put no fucking hit on yo ass nigga, you light weight I can handle you myself," Silas said.

"Yeah we see how that worked out for you last time you bitch ass nigga. Even with a gun aimed at me you gave me a bitch ass leg scratch. I shot yo ass in the stomach on purpose, I ain't wanna pop up in front of my girl."

"Oh she your girl now? I thought you would have been done with this game with her by now since clearly you see I'm not fazed by you using her to get to me. Casualties of war happen every day. She'll learn that the hard way fucking with you."

"Bitch she ain't gone learn shit as long as I'm breathing, you and whoever gotta kill me first bitch and that's on me! And that's why she ain't allowed to go around your ass, and you drop your nuts and come near my girl or my son if you want to bitch! Try me nigga! You know what I ain't with this talking bitch let's do this because I be damn if a nigga threaten my family in my face and ion see about that! Fuck you thought this was!," Legend said standing up pulling his gun out.

Cream jumped up behind him followed by me and Jaxson as Silas stood up too unbothered. His men drew their guns as we all had ours out as well. We clearly were outnumbered, but it was whatever with me. I wanted to be mature, but I was riding with my brother no matter what. Whatever decision he made, I was going with it head first.

"Look, this conversation went way left too damn fast. Now in that briefcase is the money for all of your product that was taken," I said with my gun pointed at his head as he adjusted his suit looking unbothered.

"'Money? Ok and what about my product that was confiscated by the police?"

"Nigga it don't matter about them damn drugs, you got your money for a product that we would have sold on the streets and made the same value for. I even tossed in something extra. Consider this an early payment," I said as he opened the suitcase thumbing through the bills.

"You know I can't let this shit with you slide because if I do, niggas will all start ice skating testing me and shit."

"You ain't let shit slide nigga you was paid, something yo ass been bitching about for the longest. This why this beef started," Legend said.

"You have the money so what's the deal? I didn't come at you half stepping, I brought you exactly what I owe you plus interest," I said.

"You think I give a fuck about this money? I spend more a week on my hoes," he said.

"Shit now I'll buy some hair store bundles but you got life fucked up, pussy ain't that good," Cream said.

"I fuck with bitches who got expensive taste, car, clothes, and like the finer things in life. I got enough bread to keep their asses, happy hoes, happy life. If ain't tricking if you got it," Silas said.

"Look nigga you can take the bread or give it back, but the small talk I'm done with. You been really testing my patience when I came here on some grown man shit trying to take accountability for my actions," I said.

"Shit y'all not in the position to be making demands, it's four of y'all, and a shit load of us. It's no way even if y'all got bullet proof vest on, would y'all make it out this bitch alive. So, since the balls in my court, this how this shit about to go, I'll continue to supply y'all, but y'all work for my team now, y'all not solo anymore," Silas said as Legend laughed.

"Y'all includes you as well Legend so I guess you permanently out of retirement," Silas said.

"Oh is that right?" Legend said.
"Yeah that's right, and since we practically family now, my baby shower gift to you is you can start after Gabs drop her baby."

"Naw that don't work for me," Legend said.

"Oh? Which part?" Silas smirked.

"Shit none of that," I said.

"You niggas ain't in no position to negotiate, I got the upper and here. You walking out here breathing with my offer, or you not waking out of here at all," Silas said.

"Shit, I like that ultimatum, you have the re up truck ready in five minutes, you keep the bricks at the same price, and you walk out this bitch breathing, or none of us will walk out this bitch," Legend said.

It was Silas turn to laugh then. "And what makes you think you in a position to make some fucking demands? And none of us will walk out of here? I think you smoking my product instead of selling it," Silas said.

"Look down, x marks the spot," Legend said pointing to Silas chest as he looked down at the two red sniper beams dancing across his chest. Looking around, he noticed red beams coming through the window aimed at all of his men.

"Don't worry about the men outside that were surrounding the place, they taking a nap right now. Shit we either gone all shoot each other up, or you can take our peaceful offer and get your bitch ass out my face," Legend said.

I couldn't do nothing but shake my head because I had no idea he had that shit up his sleeve. It was a couple moments of silence before Silas said,

"A truck will meet you outside with the product."

"Hell naw I ain't driving that shit this time, we'll tail them niggas back to the drop off point," I said walking past the security as I pulled my phone out making a call.

"Baby, have my pussy ready for me daddy on his way home," I said.

GABRIELA

"And like I told you guys for the hundredth time; I have no idea who that is. Gentlemen, let's be very clear here, I'm telling both of you to make this your last time contacting me. I didn't file anything missing because nothing was taken, that case is closed, and I sold that home. Right now, you guys are not doing anything but fishing for information that isn't there. This will be my last time having this pleasant conversation with you guys because the next one will be a motion that I will file with the courts," I said hanging up the phone.

That was the fifth call I've received from those detectives from that shooting that happened with Uncle Bo and Julian. They were becoming very persistent and a pain in my ass. I just wish they would drop the issue, hell they don't even put that much energy into solving real cases around the city. Picking my office phone up once more, I dialed my uncle's cell phone to check on him. I know Julian had told me to not have any contact with him, but he was my uncle, somebody who had helped raise me, how could I just not talk to him at least since they came to a peaceful understanding. Everyone thought I was crazy when I suggested a sit down, but turns out the sit down apparently worked. When he didn't answer, I gave up and got back to work. I just hoped he was ok that's all.

*****

"Damn this the second time this week my motion sensors have went off at that crib. Shit went off a few times last week as well. I think the damn sensor need to be changed or something," Julian said while we were lying in bed watching tv.

Well I was watching tv, he was on his phone.

"What crib? And do you have motions sensors at all of your

homes?" I asked him.

"Shit yeah, and all them shits hooked up to all my phones, computers and tablets," he said.

"Well who is setting it off?"

"That's the thing I don't fucking know. The camera doesn't catch them, so either it's nothing, or it's somebody who avoiding the camera," he said.

"Well did you go check it out?" I asked.

"Naw I been busy, shit it ain't shit at that crib of value I want anyways."

"Well why do you still have it? And which home is this?"

"It's the first house I ever bought that was mines. Like the first piece of property a young nigga owned. You couldn't tell me and Mike shit when we bought our brownstones," he said.

"Who is Mike?"

"Nobody important," he quickly said. I opened my mouth to say something else, but decided not to press the issue. I've learned with Julian, it was best to drop things and avoid an argument, then engage him.

"Baby we have to finalize the baby shower cake Monday at 12:30, so don't be late."

"Baby shower cake?"

"Yes, we have a final taste testing," I said.

"Man I don't give a fuck about that shit, if you undecided get both," he said.

"No baby it doesn't work like that, I can't just get both."

"How come you can't? Who gone tell you that you can't? Cuz your man said you can have whatever the fuck you want. Somebody tell you different, let me know," he said.

"Baby the purpose of this is to pick one, not to just throw money around because you don't care. I care! It's Trey's big day and my first baby shower. I want everything to be perfect," I said.

"Next year, ima be more involved than if this type of shit means that much to you. No matter what I'm doing, I'm make sure to make all of your doctor's appointments, I thought that was enough," he said.

"Next year? What's happening next year?"

"Shit ima want my daughter," he causally said like it was dumb of me to ask.

"Woah time out. You don't think one is enough for right now?"

"Yeah, and then next year we can have another one."

"Julian baby, I love you, but I just don't know if ima be in a huge rush to have another one of your big headed, feisty, ass children. Trey is constantly sitting on my bladder, and I've been miserable ever since I hit 8 months. I want my body back, and I want to build my clientele up at the law firm a little bit before I jump back into another baby," I said.

"Shit who you want ya body back for? What niggas you out here tryna look good for?" He said.

"I want it back for me, I feel like a fat cow, my face all swollen, my nose is taking up half my face, and I'm miserable and ugly. You don't even look at me the same. I'm not as sexy as I once was to you," I said finally voicing my insecurities out loud.

"Before you piss me off Gabriela, what made you think that dumb shit?"

"You haven't touched me in days, and don't say you've been tired because it's been plenty of times you've came home exhausted and yet you still woke me up for sex," I cried. It actually was really bothering me at this point more than I expected it to.

"So you think a nigga don't find you attractive? That I'm just tolerating you? Let me tell you something, I'm damn sure not with you because you carrying my seed. If that's the case it's a shit load of other rooms in this house I could lay my head in.," he said grabbing my hand putting in under the covers and bringing it down to his rock hard dick.

"You feel that? He been rocked up ready to go since I got in this damn bed with your sexy ass, and he tired of me beating his ass like I'm in elementary school or some shit. I guess I'm the only one remember your last doctor's visit when the doctor said to take it easy on everything that included sex and damn near almost kept you in the hospital a few days? Shit I'm so much of any open book when it comes to sex that at this point every muthafucka on my team both legal and illegal knows I ain't had no pussy in a few days because my damn nerves been on ten and I've had zero patience. I been shooting muthafuckas for any and no reason at all. I would hate to do the shit, but I can make myself live without sex for a while. I can't live without you and my seed. I'll sacrifice my satisfaction every time if it means Julian Santiago III is born healthy into this world and the beautiful queen who birth him is ok as well," he said making me tear up. Julian wasn't the type who expressed his feelings, so I never knew what he was thinking and feeling.

"Baby," I said as the damn broke and the tears ran down my face like water.

"Damn woman there you go with that damn crying. Yeah you right we might need to skip a year for Bella Santiago because between your ass crying and farting, I can't say shit to you or feed your ass shit either," he said causing me to laugh through my tears because my gas really had gotten bad.

But, my doctors assured me it was quite normal. Back in the day I would have died had I farted in front of Chance and I was with him over a decade. Now, I do it in front of Julian all the time because he made me feel just that comfortable with him. I also didn't think he would love me any less.

"Baby you know I can't help it when I do it," I said laughing.

"You gone shit on yourself one day watch, shitty booty ass! Yo shit be smelling worse than these niggas out here," he said.

"You a lie," I said laughing as I moved closer to him. "Baby," I said placing my hand back over his dick massaging it up and down as I heard him suck in a deep breath.

"They said for me to take it easy with my body, they didn't say anything about my mouth," I said before my head disappeared under the covers to please my man.

*****

"Y'all hoes ain't right, over here drinking knowing I want a drink. I'm ready to get out of this fucking dress because it's sticking to me," I said. I was hot and ready to go. We were current at a BBQ Block Party that Julian hosted every year at the park. All the women, children, and everyone who was anybody apparently was in attendance. This year it also doubled as a welcome home party for Case. As his brother's girlfriend, I didn't see a problem with him enjoying himself amongst family and friends. As his lawyer, I was opposed to it and wanted him to keep a very low profile. I knew the FBI was mad that I was obviously smarter than them and the games they were trying to play. They had it in their minds he was guilty before he was even processed into the facility that's why they did any and everything to prevent him from bonding out, and had been fucking with him since he's been out. I had to file several motions with the courts to get them to back down from their blatant stalking and harassing. They will throw their own case out if they keep down this path.

"Bitch you the one pregnant we not," Destiny said.

"Right I need this fucking drink to calm my nerves before I beat somebody child's ass and wait on they mammy," Stacy said.

"At the rate you and Cream fucking you gone be pregnant soon," I said. "And, you hit somebody child and you going under the jail," I said laughing.

"Ima just wait for their mammy who keep leaving their kids unattended to so they can smile all of these niggas faces. They better not show Cream not one of them teeth or I'll knock all them hoes out! And bitch the devil is a lie I catch and swallow all that nut," Stacy said.

"Bitch that's what I'm talking about," Destiny said slapping her a high five.

"Julian gone tell me he wants another baby soon as I push Trey out. I feel like he'll try and get me pregnant before my six weeks checkup. I think ima get my tubes tied behind his back," I said confessing to them something I had been contemplating for awhile

I was barely a first time mom and he was already stressing me out about putting my body through this again for another time. I just didn't think I could it. Shit I was waddling at this point, that's not attractive.

"Bitch don't get yourself in trouble doing that without talking to him first. Trust me bitch Legend gone nut the fuck up on your ass for real. You gone risk your relationship for a damn baby you can hire a nanny for?" Destiny said.

"Bitch didn't I just give you some damn advice? I said catch all that nut in your mouth so that none gets inside of you," Stacy said. *Would Julian leave me for this? I imagined him maybe being angry, but I didn't think he would leave me.*
"I just don't think I can do this shit anymore," I said crying.

"Bitch I'm sick of your ass crying. You been doing that a lot these last few weeks! Damn how you stressing bout some shit that ain't even happened yet," Destiny said.

I could admit I was more emotional than usual lately, but damn everyone didn't have to keep saying something about it.

"Y'all ain't shit! Stacy you better never get pregnant and think you gone call me," I said.

"Oh sis no fucking worries so ima stop you right there! Destiny will be pregnant before me," this idiot said.

"Bitch how? I admit I do got some good pussy the kind that make a nigga not wanna pull out, but bitch this boy pussy so how ima carry a child?" Destiny's ass shot back. I couldn't believe half the shit that came out my friends mouth sometimes.

"Exactly my point hoe! That means I'm not having one if you'll get pregnant first," Stacy said finishing her drink off and tossing it in the trash.

"Bitch how about this BBQ was mandatory for all of the workers today, that mean ima have to be out here with my boo and watch bitches all in his face," Destiny said looking stressed just thinking about it.

"Bitch what happened to the Jamaican?" I asked confused because she had seemed to really like him.

"Did he just need a green card hoe?" Stacy said.

"Hell naw that nigga said they believed in multiple wives and he was already on number 3, and was I ok with that and open to meeting them? My damn fingers couldn't tap block fast enough. I knew he was too good to be true. He wasn't afraid to show me off, made me his woman crush Wednesday every Wednesday, and randomly put money in my account," she said.

"Bitch are you a fool or a damn fool! Fuck his wives you need to be with that nigga," Stacy said.

"Usually I don't agree with Stacy but friend you tripping on that one. You don't have to marry him to continue dating him," I said.

"Yes the fuck I do, he said he ready to get married and all his wives really are women. I feel like he likes me and post me in public for appearance purposes only. How I'm the only man you've married? What if wife number five was also a woman? Like that shit too stressful, but fuck that I'm off of that dick. I'm talking about some here and now penis that's breaking my back in every chance he gets. I feel like ima embarrass myself if I see a bitch in his face," she said.

"Damn bitch you never outed one of your trades before, this dick must be serious," Stacy said.

"That big horse dick so good it'll make me spread the rumor and then snitch on my damn self," Destiny said laughing. We were currently under a shade tree but from our position, we could see the parking lot perfectly. I was in the middle of a sentence when I saw Chance walking up from the parking lot with Coco, his daughter and a group of his friends.

"Oh my God you guys what is Chance doing here?" I asked in a panic, and I didn't even know why I was panicking, nor why my heart was beating awfully fast.

"Oh he brought CoCo good because I owe that hoe an ass whopping," Stacy said takin her hair tie off her arm throwing her hair into a quick messy bun.

"Wait why?" I asked.

"Because that hoe intentional tried to hurt you when she told us it was Chanel that was fucking Chance. Matter of fact ima beating his ass too for fucking your supposed to be friend after I ask him why her of all the pussy in the world," Stacy said.

Actually I had been wondering that exact question ever since I found out. Like why Chanel? What was it about my friend that you would risk our relationship fucking her in our home. Before I could make up my mind if I seriously wanted to go over there and confront him, Stacy's ass had already taken off towards them so I had no choice but to follow behind her. Stacy wasn't the type who said what she was going to do and didn't do it. She talked her shit then followed through on it.

"Stacy no wait," I yelled after her but she reached them before I did.
"Bitch my daughter standing right here so I ain't trying to get into it with you hoes today. With a pussy that ran through, I know you wouldn't know nothing about kids and shit. But if you coming over here to fight, I'm not worried about y'all asses. My nigga finally stopped using that dumb hoe standing beside you and I beat y'all other friends ass. Shit my nigga know better now," CoCo said.

"Bitch you think I want kids? You got kids by a bum ass undercover gay ass nigga and that's something to brag on?" Stacy said as Coco turned and handed her daughter off to somebody who walked her back towards the car. I knew things were bound to go downhill from here.

"I never liked your stupid ass. Your loud ass was always jealous of Gabriela because that hot pussy can't keep a nigga to save your life. Bitch you gone die bitter with nine cats running around this bitch," Chance said.

"If the pussy good I got $40 for that hoe," John Boy, Chances best friend said.

"Bitter? Because I wanted my best friend to see and understand her worth from being with your broke dog ass. You ain't bring shit to the table nigga but a headache. I could never be bitter, but you are right I couldn't keep a nigga I never wanted to begin with. I found one I wanted though and got him on lock now," Stacy shot back.

"So that means you don't want this $40?" John Boy said as he really took $40 out of his pocket and tried to really hand it to her.

"Don't do my muthafuckin friend nigga. Keep your $40 your dick damn sure ain't worth $1," Destiny said.

"Damn," everybody who had gathered around us said.

"Damn Destiny how you know," Stacy said.

"Girl I sampled that $1 dick and was real pissed off girl. Nigga was acting like he was King Kong but really I got a baby turtle," she said.

"Nigga I ain't never touched shit that looked like you. I'll beat you like the nigga you was born," John Boy said getting hype as he and Destiny started arguing.

The whole time I was still processing what Coco had said to me. I don't know what came over me but I said,

"Bitch he knows better now huh? So I guess that's why he been blowing the skin off my inbox on Facebook because he knows better? Right? He with you because I won't take his ass back bitch so you are welcome," I said as her eyes got big probably from the shock of me actually standing up for myself.

I was on a roll now so I turned to him and said,
"And you fucked my friend in my fucking bed though? What the fuck did I ever do to your broke ass that was that bad that of all the pussy in the world, you chose her to sleep with?" I said.

"Broke? Bitch I could never be broke, I just kept my money and spent your shit. And I fucked her cuz she threw the pussy at me and because I could. Shit you wouldn't have done anything about it if you knew about it just like you knew I was still fucking with my baby momma," he said.

"Nigga you was broke, and dusty that's why I upgraded your ass that's why you still driving that old ass Benz I bought you bitch nigga," I said pointing to the car "And you can have that bitch and any bitch you want because you cheating on me was the best thing that could have happened to me. I found out every nigga don't have a dick that won't come past his balls. Some actually blessed with a dick from Wakanda. I also upgraded from a worker to a boss something you Coco will never know about because my baby's dick will be bigger than the dick you getting and his ass will forever be a worker," I said rubbing my stomach.

I really just wanted to hurt them as much as they hurt me so I was saying anything at this point.

"Damn my bitch said her baby's dick is bigger than your nigga's dick! Sis that's terrible! I feel so bad for you," Stacy said not making it no better as she burst out laughing. It was a small crowd gathered around us now and her laugh was contagious as everyone else began to laugh as well.

"Just because a nigga nutted in that wack ass pussy don't make him your nigga bitch. Don't get beside yourself because I'll crush your dreams with one phone call," CoCo said pausing me as Stacy reached over me and punched her dead in her face at the same time that John Boy and Destiny started fighting. Thing is she really looked like a female though like fully, so the minute he swung on her, niggas jumped in to help her beating his ass as his friends tried to help him.

"Bitch don't get comfortable with that fuck nigga cuz both y'all asses living on borrowed time," Chance said mushing the top of my forehead. Before I could react, his body dropped. Literally dropped because Julian came out of nowhere and hit him one time dropping his body.

"Nigga you done lost your muthafucka mind putting your hands on her!" Julian roared. He was madder than I've seen him in a long time.

CAUGHT UP IN A DOPEBOY' LOVE 2

"That bitch brought her ugly ass over here all in his face! You wait until you drop that baby it's on sight bitch," Coco yelled out at me walking over to
Chance.

"Bitch any smoke you got for her ima catch all that shit," Stacy yelled trying to break free from the hold Cream had on her.

I didn't even notice them walking up. Chance pushed Coco off him who was trying to help him up as he got back on his feet then rushed Julian. They started fighting and even though Chance was hurt, he was hanging in there a little bit but he was really no match for Julian. Somehow the guys broke them apart and was holding tight onto each other them.

"Naw let that bitch go," Julian said.

"Nigga I ain't scared of you, bitch ass nigga. You don't pump fear in my chest like these other niggas and you know this already," Chance said struggling to get free.

"This ain't what you want bitch nigga," Julian said.

"It's exactly what I want nigga," Chance said.

"Chance you not even like that nigga. Take you, them weak ass niggas you came with and that raggedy bitch and get y'all asses on. Effective immediately I ain't getting down with you like that no more," Case said.

"It's always money over bitches right? But yo brother in his chest cuz I fucked his bitch before. Fuck yo team nigga I was on my way out the door anyway," Chance said.
Why he said that I don't know because it's like Julian got super human strength as he tossed the men holding him off of him and charged towards Chance. As soon as he made it to him however, bullets rang out as everybody dropped to the ground. Julian immediately ran to me and dove on top of me.

"Who bussing?" He yelled to Cream as some niggas started shopping back, while others were on the ground as well. As soon as the shooting started, it had stopped. As Julian helped me to my feet, he looked around noticing Chance had disappeared.

"You fucked that nigga?" Julian said walking up on me.

"No, well yes that's my ex fiancé. But I didn't know he would be here or that he even worked for you," I said to him.

"What you in that night face for?"

"I wanted to know why he slept with Chanel," I said.

"Why the fuck that bullshit matters when you carrying my fucking seed and sleeping beside me every night. You must still want that nigga," he said walking off.

"No it's not like that I promise you Julian I love you," I said pulling on his shirt. He just snatched away from me however and kept walking. **What the hell just happened?**

****

"Can you tell Cream to tell Julian that I haven't spoken to Chance since we broke up," I said to Stacy. After everything that happened at the park yesterday, Julian still wasn't talking to me. We argued some more when we got home, and then for the first time since we've been living together, I slept alone.

"Girl I'm already in the dog house my damn self for fighting CoCo and being in Chance face and you want me to bring this nigga name back up to Cream? Did you not forget what happened last time?" She said referring to when he killed a man in front of her.

"I know but Julian won't talk to me at all. He literally leaves all my text messages on read," I whined.

"Bitch nobody told yo ass to run behind me. I was just gone beat the bitch ass and dip. All that extra ass conversation that happened was unnecessary. You knew Legend wasn't going for that shit. Then to have another man tell you they fucked yo bitch like that, yeah bitch you gone be sucking dick until you catch lock jaw to make it up to that nigga," Stacy said all loudly not even caring that we were inside of a bakery.

When Julian didn't come to my cake tasting appointment, I called Stacy and she agreed to meet me up here. Thankfully they were still letting us in here even though my appointment was for an hour ago.

"This strawberry one right here bomb sis," she said.

"I like this butter cream one," I said.

"So you think I can seduce my way back into his good graces?"

"Pussy might not be enough, you gone have to pull out all the stops and your ass too big to be trying something kinky."

"You the main one was just telling me I need to give him head, now sex might not be enough?"

"Bitch I don't know, don't listen to my advice, I can only deal with one psycho at a time. Shit I really only know how to tame mines, you on your own with Legends ass. I would hate to see what he gone do to Chance, but I bet you gone have front row seats like I did," she said as I shuttered at the thought.

Would Julian really kill Chance in front of me? I know I hated him with a passion, but was I really ready to watch him die?

****

"We're closed," I said getting up from my desk as I heard my door bell ding alerting me that someone was inside of my law firm. I had thought I locked the door when I came to my desk. I had no intentions of being here long, I just needed to grab some information for Case because we had court coming up next week. Holding my stomach that had been bothering me all day, I made my way to the front.

"I'm sorry, I am closed for the day, but if you leave your name," my voice trailed off as I made it to the front coming face to face with the last person I ever thought I would see again.

"What are you doing here Burt?" I said rolling my eyes at the asshole not bothering to hide the fact that I didn't want to see him. He was the main reason I had quit my job.

"Nice to see you too Gabriela. I guess the mystery of you being sick is solved. Bummer, I thought it was drugs making you sick, who knew it was a baby," his ugly pigeon faced ass said.

"You son of a bitch, get off my property."

"This is a nice little space that you have here," he continued talking.

"Yeah a space that I have, that's mines. A board can't vote me out, now take you, and that cheat ass cologne that's fucking with my stomach and get out of my shit," I said.

"Somebody got pregnant and got a nasty attitude. But listen the reason I'm here isn't for a damn social call. I'm looking for my brother," he was saying until I cut him off.

"I never even knew you had siblings, but you need a private investigator or some shit. Not me, goodbye Burt , tell Pete I hope he gets hit by a car," I said.

"I'm looking for my brother, he's missing, well the official report is he just up and left, but I know that's a lie. I started looking into some of his files and what he was last working on which is what led me to this dump. His old client is your new client."

"What are you talking about?"

"Case Santiago, that's your new client according to court documents and that's also the last thing that Malechi was working on before he disappeared without a trace," he said as I felt the room beginning to spin.

LEGEND

"How hard is it to find one muthafucka?" I said pissed off because nobody knew where this nigga Chance was at.

"Shit we been by his crib he share with his baby momma and his moms crib, that nigga ain't there. Shit his crib was empty when we went there and it's no way he could have cleared that shit out that fucking fast. That nigga had to have been planning something for a while now," Jaxson said.

"Snatch his homies up, I want everybody who was with him at the park dead," I said sitting down in my chair. It was something about what that nigga said that replayed in my mind again. He said he was on his way out anyway. Ain't nobody gone say no shit like that unless they had some shit up their sleeve. I can't believe this the nigga that fucked my bitch, like the more I thought about it, the more I couldn't wait to kill this nigga. I couldn't believe she was sitting in that nigga face asking him why he fucked her homegirl like that shit mattered. It's shit like that that made me wanna revert back to my old ways, like that's some foul ass sneaky shit. I got something for that ass though, she gone learn I'm not the nigga to fuck with. And now that I know that's the nigga she used to fuck with, I definitely need her ass to know I'm not that bitch ass nigga!
RING RING

My phone began to ring as I quickly answered it.

"Talk to me you found out who that was shooting at us at the park yet?" I asked Hal because we still had no fucking clue who started bussing. Cream chalked it up to some random niggas shooting into the crowed because that's typically how it goes in the hood. But, everybody out there knew that was my event, ain't nobody that fucking crazy to let off rounds randomly anywhere I'm at. At first I thought it was Silas trying to get back at us because of how we got back in business with him. But it made no sense if it was him because nobody was hit at all, the shit was real sloppy.

"No I hacked into the street cameras newsfeed but I didn't get much from them. Each angle never caught the shooter, or a shooter at all, only people running and shooting back into the air at nothing. I will definitely keep looking. But that's not why I was calling you. I'm calling because I finally cracked into the FBI system. They had so many damn fire walls up, but I'm in. So it turns out Case wasn't anywhere on the FBI's radar until the day he got locked up," Hal said.

"So they just got lucky when they stopped him? Bullshit."

"No they intentionally stopped him. It turns out a nigga named Rodger was pulled over for drunk driving and they found a bag of weed on him, and he had a few warrants for his arrest. He is the one who told them about Case and the shipment he was driving down," Hal said.

So Case was set up because this nigga ain't want to take the lil 6 months he would have gotten for them drugs. Whole time I thought Case was out here wildin' and that's why he got caught up.

"Bet find that nigga for me," I said to Hal before I hung up the phone with him and called Case up. I filled him in on everything as I grabbed my keys headed out to meet him at the warehouse.

****

"I fucking knew it! I told yo ass I wasn't out here slipping like that! Damn I knew it was something!" Case said pacing back and forth.

"I can't believe Rodger's bitch ass turned snitch over a fucking dime bag," I said.

"Where his ass at, let's go," Case said.

"Nigga he an informant for the Feds, probably the only nigga who can put you away, you think he ain't in witness protection under surveillance? Look how they been on yo ass since you got out," I said.

"Naw I think I saw that nigga the other day," Cream said.

"Even if he ain't ask for the shit, don't mean they ain't watching. Once you get in bed with the feds, ain't no going back. Fuck," I said because who knows what all Rodger's ass had been telling them, and if he's been wearing a wire sitting in on meetings and shit.

"We gotta shut everything down again. This nigga probably gave these bitch ass niggas an opening to build a case on all of our asses. I ain't doing no time for this nigga. We need to be smart about how we move from this point on," I said.

"Fuck," Cream said as the reality of what I said finally hit him as he punched a wall.

"Man this shit fucked up," Case said. "If they got something on us, ima take the fall for everything."

"No the fuck you won't!" I yelled jumping up and getting in his face. I knew I had a son to think about now, but I be damn if I watch my baby brother do a life bid for some shit I brought him into. Rodger a nigga from my old team, so technically it's my slip up for not noticing his snake ass tendencies sooner and deading that nigga.

"They found JohnBoy," Jaxson said walking into where we were.

"I need him brought to me alive," I said before I turned back to Case,

"You not taking the fall for this shit, believe that," I said.

*****

"So how you was just with that nigga the other day but claim you don't know where he at?" I asked John Boy as Cream sliced him across his chest causing him to yell out again like a bitch. He had so much mouth the other day and was this tough guy, but now he was crying and pissing on his self. Niggas like him disgusted me.

"Man I promise on my baby life I don't know where that fool at. We split up after we left the park and I haven't heard from him since," he said.

"You promise on your baby?" I said as I walked over to the door and opened it as one of my men brought his baby momma and his daughter inside.

"Daddy," the little girl said trying to run to him as her mother held on tightly to her.

"Fuck Legend please bro I'm begging you please, I'll tell you anything you need to know, please don't do this! Fuck!" He said struggling to break lose.

"See bitch ass niggas like you think I'm something y'all can play with until they learn the hard fucking way that I'm the last nigga you wanna take it there with. I know for a fact I seen Rodger with y'all asses a few times. So cut the bullshit and start talking before I put both of their asses down right now," I said aiming my gun at his girl and baby. Usually women and children were off limits to me, not all the time, but usually.

"Ok ok we had nothing to do with that nigga Rodger snitching like a bitch but Chance did tell him to give the Feds the route information on Case so that they could hit him that night," he said.

"What the fuck so y'all niggas been plotting on me on the low after I put y'all on and made sure you bitches was eating good!" Case said walking over and punching John Boy so hard his teeth flew out of his mouth.

"I got this chill," I said to Case.

"Man that wasn't me, that was that man!" John Boy said.

"Shit that's yo best friend, I'm sure you was right there when he said the shit, so you guilty by association bitch ass nigga. You think cuz you ain't the one who said it you ain't guilty? But what else happened I know that's not all. What else y'all do?" I said because it was looking like they set Case up the whole time to take the fall so they had to have an end game.

"The same night Case got hit up, we hit the warehouse for the rest of the drugs that was left over. But I ain't seen that shit since we took it I put this on everything I love bruh. The plan was to get Case out the way and take over, but shit Chance was taking more and more trips out of town but he never once told me when we was gone go with our move. Shit he played me too then if y'all saying he cleared his house out. I ain't know nothing about this shit," John Boy said.

"Basically yo bitch ass let a nigga use you, and then left you to take the fall. That nigga knew I was coming for him, so his ass got ghost, and didn't tell yo ass to get lost too. Shit you really played yo self because after what happened, any other nigga would have been left," I said.

"Where he been taking trips to?" Case asked as something suddenly came to me.

"Y'all the ones hit our traps huh?" I said.

"Yeah," JohnBoy said. Shit was crazy because the whole time I'm thinking it was Silas fucking with me when it's been these niggas that was right under my nose all along. But that doesn't explain Jamaica? Like a bitch ass nigga like Chance couldn't have pulled no shit like that off, could he?

"Nigga ima ask you this one time and one time only, y'all burnt my momma house down?"

"Hell no! I don't even know your momma or where she stay at in Atlanta," he said.

I knew then they definitely ain't have nothing to do with Jamaica or he would have mentioned Jamaica not Atlanta. So Silas still the prime suspect on that incident. I had a lot of shit to think about, and I was done chit chatting with this nigga. Walking over to his baby momma, I put two bullets into her head as he yelled out,

"What the fuck! Why would you do that! I told you everything you asked me! Noo Christina no!" He said as he broke down crying.

"Nigga you put it on your baby's life that you was telling the truth, you ain't said nothing about yo bitch, I thought her life wasn't important to you my fault folk," I said nodding my head as Cream lit his ass up like the Fourth of July.

I walked off with even more questions than answers as I tried to wrap my brain around this Chance situation. How long this nigga been plotting on me and did Gabriela really not know about it?

*****

"Where you at?" Cream said.

I'm driving to my old brownstone," I said.

"What you going there for?"

"The damn motion sensors keep going off but when I pull up the camera, I don't see shit. It's probably some lil bad ass kids from the neighborhood walking by or some shit," I said.

"Yeah you might need to change the batteries or really you need to gone sell that shit. I don't know what the fuck you holding on for," he said.

"Cuz it's my shit bitch," I said laughing.

"Anyway, man that shit back there was crazy, but I don't think sis knew anything that nigga was doing," Cream said.

"What?" I said.

"Nigga I know you and I know how you get. That girl loves your ugly ass, I don't know why she do, but she do. She done proved herself over and over again that she down to ride. Whatever that nigga been planning, she didn't t know about it," Cream said.

"I hear you," I said pulling into the driveway of the first house I called home.

"You hear me but are you listening to me?"

"Silas always said he ain't send no hit on my momma, and when I mentioned the shit to him at Gabriela's crib now that I think about it, he looked surprised as fuck," I said changing the subject.

"If he ain't get at yo momma, then who did? Chance damn sure ain't got enough money and muscle to pull off the shit they did. Who else we had beef with at that time besides Silas?"

"I don't know, shit just not adding up but ima get to the bottom of all this shit soon," I said getting out of the car walking up to the front door.

I hung up the phone with him as I put my key in and walked inside as memories of the past instantly hit me. I haven't laid my head in this house since the night I killed Mike. It wasn't much inside of the house since I had my niggas clear it out, and whatever they didn't take, I damn sure didn't want. I usually have cleaning services come in and clean all of my spots either weekly or bi weekly, but this was the only one nobody was allowed to touch. You would think since I didn't get it cleaned, and didn't give a fuck about it, that I would be quick to sell it but

I just wasn't. I don't know why but it just reminded me to never forget where I came from and the sacrifices I had to make and all the hard work it took. Shit, I was up night and day busting my ass in these streets to buy this brownstone in cash.

Walking around the living and dining room area, I didn't see anything suspicious as I walked upstairs. I was trying to see if I saw any broken windows where maybe some kids might have thrown rocks inside. Anything that would have caused the motion sensors to go off. When I didn't see any broken in any of the two rooms, I headed towards the master bedroom as I got a text on my phone right before it started ringing. Noticing it was Gabriela, I let it go to voicemail, but when she called me again, I answered it and all I heard was screaming. Instantly becoming alert, I said,

"What's wrong? You ok? Where you at?"

"It's the baby, Trey is coming I just texted you my location. GET HERE NOW," she screamed.

"Fuck I'm on my way, hold on," I said as my heart beat sped up, my palms became sweaty and I suddenly felt light headed. I was really about to be a daddy. All I could think about was getting to my family as quick as possible as I raced out of the room and down the stairs. Throwing the front door open, their blocking my way stood the last person I ever expected to see again in this lifetime.

"What the fuck you doing here Myriah?" I said instantly becoming engaged.

I know this whole time it ain't been her stupid ass setting the motion sensors off. Since she knew where all the cameras were, it did make sense and explained why I never seen anything.

" I gotta go. Get the fuck out of my way before I kill your stupid ass," I said as I noticed for the first time a little boy standing beside her. Following my gaze, she said,

"Legend, meet Julian Santiago III, your son."

TOO BE CONTINUED....

NOTE FROM THE AUTHOR

"Phillipians 4:13 I can do ALL things through Christ who strengthens me. That's what I kept telling myself as I pushed through and finished this book. From the bottom of my heart I thank each and every one of you who took the time to read this release. I am excited to embark on this new journey in life continuing to stay steadfast and unmoving in the Lord. Because after all, if God is for you who can be against you? I encourage each of you to ALWAYS trust yourself and your craft. To believe in YOU when no one else does. To be your own motivator, and loudest cheerleader. If you understand time and season than know that ITS OK if it's not your time nor season. However, until God opens both of those doors for you, continue to praise him in the hallway! Your best is yet to come! As always, you guys can follow me on all of my social media pages listed below.

Facebook personal page @Jasmine Miller-Smith

Facebook author page @Author Carmen Lashay

Readers page@Lashay With The Pen Slay

Backup readers page @Author Carmen Lashay's Reading Group

Instagram personal page@Pardon_My_Pretti_

Instagram author page@AuthorCarmenLashay

Snapchat@Married&Bougie

ABOUT THE AUTHOR

Author Carmen Lashay born Jasmine Miller, is a native of Monroe, Louisiana. The young author has since relocated to Tx where she continued her studies at Texas A&M University Commerce graduating in May 2019, and returning to school for the fall to continue furthering her education. The national bestselling author has written over 26 novels and doesn't see herself slowing down anytime soon. Carmen Lashay has been in love with books since her 4th grade teacher, Mrs. Joyner, introduced the class to Harry Potter and the Sorcerer's Stone. Since then her love for books has blossomed into a passion for reading as well as writing. In her spare time, she enjoys traveling, thrift shopping, binge watching shows such as Criminal Minds and Big Bang Theory, and relaxing at home with a glass of wine and her kindle. Carmen Lashay hopes to produce books that will capture the hearts and attention of readers all over the world, as well as keep them on the edge of their seats coming back to enjoy more stories.

Made in the USA
Columbia, SC
07 January 2024